Ociee on Her Own

Ociee on Her Own

A Novel

Milam McGraw Propst

[signature: Milam McGraw Propst]

Mercer University Press
Macon

ISBN 0-86554-838-2
MUP/H631

© 2003 Mercer University Press
6316 Peake Road
Macon, Georgia 31210-3960
All rights reserved

First Edition.

∞The paper used in this publication meets the minimum requirements
of American National Standard for Information Sciences—
Permanence of Paper for Printed Library Materials, ANSI Z39.48-
1992.

Library of Congress Cataloging-in-Publication Data

Propst, Milam McGraw.
 Ociee on her own : a novel / Milam McGraw Propst.—
1st ed.
    p. cm.
ISBN 0-86554-838-2 (alk. paper)
1. Girls—Fiction. 2. Motherless families—Fiction.
3. Asheville (N.C.)—Fiction. 4. Mississippi--Fiction. I.
Title.
 PS3566.R676O26 2003
 813'.54—dc21
                                    2003005533

This, my third book, is dedicated to my family: to my husband Jamey and our children, Amanda, William, and Jay, along with William's wife Abigail and their precious child, our grandson, Loftin Alan Propst. Born December 17, 2001, Loftin is the first great, great-grandchild of Ociee Nash Whitman.

Ociee on Her Own

1

"Elizabeth Murphy, you are my very best friend in all of North Carolina, but I do declare, you can be so lazy!" I dipped my brush in the whitewash and splashed more paint on the front seat of Mr. Lynch's carriage.

"I am not lazy, Ociee Nash!" She frowned at me. "I'm cold is all."

Ignoring her complaint, I pleaded, "Oh, Elizabeth, please get busy or we won't be done when Mr. Lynch comes by to get his buggy."

"I'm busy enough, Ociee. Fact is I'm freezing almost to death. See how the whitewash is frozen to my brush?" She tried to prove that by showing how the bristles wouldn't bend.

"The paint is *drying* because you're going too slow. Come on, girl, quit being such a pokey priss."

"All right, I'll keep working," groused Elizabeth. "But I'm no priss!"

"I know that."

With that, I got too much whitewash on my own brush and paint dripped down into the right sleeve of my winter coat. I spun around so Elizabeth wouldn't see and backed into the wet carriage.

"Looks like you're getting as much whitewash on you as on the buggy," snickered Elizabeth.

I stuck out my tongue.

My friend and I were as different as daytime and night. To begin with, we actually looked the opposite. My hair was a mop of curly blond frizz that shot out in a thousand directions. My eyes were soft gray to match my light complexion. A light complexion exactly like Mama's, it was.

Elizabeth had darker skin, olive in color, with the deepest darkest brown eyes. Her shiny black hair was as straight as a fireplace poker. Mrs. Murphy could comb Elizabeth's hair in the morning, and it would stay that way all the day long. I was jealous of her hair, but she was jealous of my age.

I was eleven. Elizabeth was still only ten. Of course, she was quick to tell whoever would listen that she'd turn eleven soon enough. Her birthday was in January, two whole months after mine. I'd been eleven since way back in November. That made her as mad as mad could be, especially since Elizabeth knew she could never catch up with me.

If I told the honest-to-goodness truth about the things heaviest in my heart, I'd have to admit that I was jealous of her, too. I was jealous of Elizabeth because she had a mother. My Mama was dead.

"Drat!" I dripped more paint on my coat. I wrinkled my forehead and sucked air in through my teeth. "Aunt Mamie's gonna get me for this."

"Best go slowly, Ociee, and try to paint more care-fulllly," drawled Elizabeth as she dotted my nose with her brush. I whipped around and spattered some paint on her cheek. Elizabeth quickly re-dipped her brush and slung it at me.

I retaliated. "Take that, care-fulllly."

"And another helping for you, Miss Priss!" shouted Elizabeth.

Before either of us realized it, we were battling like a couple of those awful boys at our school. Wet and nasty as could be, we rolled down onto the walkway. With the cold all but forgotten, we held our stomachs and laughed wildly. "Ociee, we're whitewashed enough that we match that buggy!"

"Elizabeth, I'm glad Mr. Lynch stabled Old Horse for the morning, or else he'd look like a ghost horse!" We giggled all the more.

My best friend and I were opposites on our insides, too. Elizabeth was cautious and slow to make decisions. It wasn't in her nature to have a whitewash fight, at least not before Ociee Nash arrived in Asheville. I expect I was considered a bad influence on Elizabeth.

I'd try almost anything without thinking very long about it. Aunt Mamie and Papa were fairly concerned about that particular trait of mine. They termed my courage "almost dangerous," but that didn't worry me in the least. I was far more interested in discovering new things than I was in being prudent. I'd learned about courage from my brothers, especially from Ben, who was a year older than me. An occasional bump or setback never had stopped a Nash, and I wasn't going to let anything stop me just because I was a girl.

As we rested, I caught sight of our old Miss Kitty Cat dozing on the porch roof. There she was soaking in the sunshine with not one thing to disturb her morning nap. There Elizabeth and I were, covered in whitewash, having worked ourselves into a near tizzy. It was certain that Miss Kitty Cat had not earned herself a ride in the upcoming parade. I acknowledged that Elizabeth had.

Our neighborhood planned a grand parade to welcome 1900 and the brand new century. With only three days left until January 1, I realized the event would be upon us before we could blink. That was enough to make me anxious. Also, as nice as Mr. Lynch was to allow Elizabeth and me to decorate his buggy for the parade, he had made it perfectly clear that we were to finish what we were doing by noon. He didn't want to miss those good fares over the busy weekend.

George Lynch was my Aunt Mamie's beau. In fact, they met because of me.

Mr. Lynch told folks, "I'd have never won the heart of Mamie Nash without the help of her niece, Ociee." Aunt Mamie wasn't ready to admit he'd won, not just yet anyhow; but he kept saying so just the same. My aunt would roll her eyes and say, "You hush up, George!"

Mr. Lynch was the very first friend I made in Asheville.

On the second day of September in 1898, I traveled all by myself on the train from Abbeville, Mississippi, to Asheville, North Carolina. I was only nine years old. When I got off the train, Mr. Lynch and his fine Old Horse took me to Aunt Mamie's house at 66 Charlotte Street.

I was surely hoping Aunt Mamie would say yes to marrying Mr. Lynch.

Elizabeth stood up, brushed the leaves and grass off her coat and said, "Admit it, Ociee Nash." Her hands on her hips, she pursed her lips. "You *are* cold!"

"Am not!" I waved my brush at her and paint flew into her hair.

The front door swung open, and my aunt called, "Ociee, what on earth are you young ladies up to now? And what's all over you? Is that whitewash?"

"Just decorating the buggy for the parade is all," said I.

Looking like a stack of wobbling velvet pillows, my aunt scurried down the porch steps. She pinned her salt and pepper hair into place as she got to us. "I've been in the back of the house sewing. All of a sudden, I just knew you girls were up to mischief."

"Not us!"

"Oh, no, not Ociee Nash and Elizabeth Murphy." My aunt began to wipe my face with the hem of her apron. "Gracious sakes alive," she uttered again and again as she attempted to scrub us both clean. "I suppose that's the best I can do without soap and water. Now let me see what you girls have done with George's carriage."

"What do you think so far?" I asked as she inspected our efforts. "Oh, Aunt Mamie, it's nearly noon. Mr. Lynch will be along any minute!"

"Hmmm, I see."

Elizabeth and I looked sheepishly at one another.

"Of course, we still need to put on the decorations—the bows, the bells; and we'll add the holly sprigs. Aunt Mamie, will you help us a little bit, so we can finish it quickly, oh, please!" My aunt eyed me. I wasn't sure what her answer would be.

Mamie Nash had run a seamstress shop in her home for nearly twenty years. She had taught me about doing things in a "flawless" manner, often emphasizing the word *flawless*. Flawless was her absolute standard for the fancy hats and beautiful clothes she created for her devoted customers. Not only did my aunt teach me about sewing, but she also cautioned me about pleasing folks, even those she termed somewhat "persnickety." She frequently commented, "People tend to take notice of what's wrong, long before they notice the first thing about what's right." To my way of thinking, on that particular morning anyhow, my aunt's high standards should have applied to decorating carriages.

"Of course, of course I will. Let's get busy, girls. The sooner we are finished here, the sooner you two can get cleaned up."

I passed the basket full of holly to her. "See, Aunt Mamie, we've shined the leaves with butter just as you taught me to do."

"Very good, Ociee."

Just like Elizabeth forgot the cold, Aunt Mamie overlooked the whitewash we'd spilled everywhere. As the three of us worked together, Mr. Lynch's buggy was wonderfully transformed into a fairytale carriage bathed in whitewash and covered with gold ribbons, silver bells, and shiny green holly sprigs.

Elizabeth said, "I'm sorry, Ociee, but you need to know that most people aren't going to all this much trouble for the parade."

"Elizabeth, you and I are not 'most people!' *We* are special," I argued emphatically. "Mr. Lynch and Aunt Mamie are special, too. And we four will be riding in a very *special* buggy, if I have my say about things."

Elizabeth sighed and smirked. Aunt Mamie smiled.

I added, "And don't forget this either. Old Horse is the very finest of all the carriage horses in Asheville. He deserves to be harnessed to the most flawlessly decorated buggy in the parade!"

Elizabeth was silenced.

"Oh, I almost forgot! Since we've been talking about Old Horse, I have something to show you, Elizabeth." I winked at my aunt and said, "I'll be right back." As I hurried up the steps, I turned. "Please, while I'm inside, try to finish tying on those bells, Elizabeth. Aunt Mamie, the holly, oh pleeease!"

Elizabeth groaned. Aunt Mamie laughed, adding, "Be careful not to drip on my floor, child!"

Mama died in the measles epidemic when I was eight years old. A year later, I left our farm in Mississippi and came to live with my aunt. Papa believed his sister Mamie could teach me how to be more ladylike. I was more prone to jumping on moving trains and chasing gypsies. Besides, Papa hadn't been schooled in feminine things. He said in a letter to his sister,

> *Mamie, dear, I suppose you would be a better teacher for my Ociee girl than is your rugged old brother. I will have to ponder this for a while, however.*
> *Yours truly, George Nash.*

Although Papa claimed that he wanted me to go, when I got ready to leave, he was sick at heart. He, my brothers Ben and Fred, and I near about fell to pieces at the depot when we said goodbye.

As miserable as I was about leaving my family and mighty scared, too, it was even worse once I got to Aunt Mamie's. I missed my family something awful. Our farm in Marshall County might as well have been way across the Atlantic Ocean, it seemed so far away to me. And being away from them made missing Mama all the worse.

Even so, things had worked out pretty well in some ways. I was "a charming young lady," folks said. I liked Asheville and Aunt Mamie. I liked Elizabeth, too. Papa and the boys had done all right, too, or so they tried to convince me.

I took the stairs two at a time and scampered down the hall to my room. There it was on the window seat, my great-grandfather's black silk top hat. Aunt Mamie had helped me spruce it up with a spanking new silver ribbon around the brim. We'd tied the ribbon into a big bow, leaving enough to stream down Old Horse's long, thick, golden mane. I'd added a magnificent wispy, bright yellow feather, one my aunt had set aside to make a fancy bonnet.

"The perfect touch," Aunt Mamie had praised me. I was a little worried that she might scold me for "wasting" the feather. But she didn't. She attached a strap so we could secure the hat under Old Horse's jaw. She and I meant for that horse to look as handsome as any gentleman in our parade.

"Turn of the Century," I carefully penned the words in my black leather-bound journal. I always kept it on the table beside my bed. Quickly I scribbled, *Noon Friday, carriage is almost ready. Details about our decorations will be added later.*

On the page before, I'd written a longer entry: *The old century shouldn't turn too gently. It should sail high across the sky like a shooting star to announce the new century's birth. I hope and pray that 1900 will cover me and all of us Nashes with a blanket of happy blessings. Surely nothing else sad will touch me or my folks.*

I was wishing that much of 1897, 1898, and 1899 and the terrible events that those years brought could be washed clean out of my memory the very second the new century was born. I gently touched Mama's picture.

I loved Aunt Mamie, but I did so miss Papa. And as much as I enjoyed Elizabeth, even she couldn't fill up the hole my heart saved for Papa, for Ben and Fred, and for Mama. I truly cared for Elizabeth's folks, too, and along with them, for all the friends I'd made in Asheville, especially Mr. Lynch and Old Horse. But the Ociee in me couldn't help but to yearn for my real home.

Aunt Mamie tried to explain that strong roots never really let go of a person like me. "Ociee, you are a very sensitive person. You have a great gift, one which you will eventually learn to treasure."

"Why does my gift have to hurt so much?"

"Because it's growing ever deeper, dearest."

I wanted to understand. Maybe I did. I knew my roots had a mighty long way to stretch, all the way from my home in Marshall County, Mississippi, to 66 Charlotte Street in Asheville, North Carolina.

I was almost afraid ask my aunt if the roots that bound me to Mama would ever let loose.

2

Old Horse's hat atop my head, I slid down the banister squealing, "Happy New Year!"

Aunt Mamie hurried to catch me. "I declare, child, do be careful!" One arm clutching me, she motioned for Elizabeth to come inside. "And you dear, you must get warm. Leave your wet coat on the hall tree."

"Yes, ma'am." Elizabeth caught sight of the hat and burst out laughing. "Ociee, silly goose, you look like a circus clown!"

I laughed at that. "The hat belonged to my great-grandfather Nash. Aunt Mamie and I fixed it up for Old Horse to wear on Monday. It's just grand, Elizabeth, don't you think?"

She giggled, "I think *you* should wear it."

"Old Horse, Elizabeth! The hat is for Old Horse!"

Aunt Mamie shook her head, then winked and said, "I have a little surprise that should settle that question. While you two were outside painting, I finished a dress for Ociee to wear in the parade."

"For me, Aunt Mamie?"

"Yes, dear girl. We'll let Old Horse keep the hat."

"Mamie Nash, Seamstress Shop" had been bustling for months as my aunt, her helpers, and I created party dresses, ball gowns, and festive clothing for the 1899 holiday season. In fact, for the first time ever, Aunt Mamie had hired assistants. Lavonia and Opal began working in July.

They were the eighteen-year-old twin sisters of Daisy Nell, the cook for the McCalls, a couple who lived next door to us. The three girls had grown up in the Blue Ridge Mountains, and I was absolutely fascinated with them. Besides Daisy Nell, I'd never known other real mountain people. To top that, I'd never seen any twins close up. Of course, I knew there were such people. My older brother Fred once met a set of matching men in Abbeville. Ben and I made him tell us all about them as soon as he got home.

"The one named Clem would only talk when the other one, Clyde, hushed," began Fred. "Clyde said he was birthed first, so it stood to reason he had to be the man to speak first. The two of them walked exactly alike, raised their left arms at the same time, and even had identical neck twitches! They looked like one another, too, except for one thing; Clem, I think it was, had a beard. I figured that was to help their people to tell which from which."

I wrote my family about the mountain twins. The twin part was only the beginning of what was interesting about them. As cold as it would get, neither of them ever wore shoes in our house. The exception was if a customer was coming by, then Aunt Mamie would insist on the shoes. The twins would reluctantly agree, but they would walk around real gentle-like, as if they were afraid they might wear a hole in the floor.

"Shoes orta be saved for the out-of-doors cold!" Opal insisted. "Girl, they's jist wasted on these purday rugs, and besides, they ache our toes sumthin' fierce."

The sisters were very thin with waist-length, brown braided hair. Of course, neither had a beard like Clem, or was it Clyde? I couldn't tell which twin was which until I noticed the one difference. Opal's right eye was gray, and the left one was brown. I never saw anything as strange. I asked her, "Miss Opal, do you see different colors out of each eye?"

She laughed out loud at me. But before she could answer, Aunt Mamie told me to hush up. She took me aside and explained I had been impolite by calling attention to Opal's oddity. I felt truly sorry about that because I liked Opal and wouldn't have hurt her for anything.

"Sorry about your eye, er, about saying anything," I stammered.

"Twern't nothing," said Opal. "Why they's folks back home that say I'm a witch. Theys call it 'Opal's evil eye'!"

"A witch!"

Aunt Mamie gave me her own version of an evil eye. I quieted myself and watched the girls cut out the satin fabric for a customer's dress. It occurred to me that perhaps my train had passed right by the sisters' home place that day I came up through the mountains. Assuming there wasn't anything impolite about that kind of question, I asked.

Lavonia answered, "Likely not, darlin', we's pretty well hid up thar."

They both knew a good bit about Indians and spirits, about bears and the caves where they slept the whole winter long. I learned about snakes, too. The girls insisted some snakes could swim straight up a waterfall! "Them snakes have to set their minds to it though," explained Opal. "Can't all of them jist go and do it. Reckon they's like people thataway."

Opal also taught me about all kinds of strange critters, some which prowled around in the night and could see through pitch black dark. Sometimes, I got out of breath just listening. I really loved to talk with those twins. My time with them was even more significant after they hinted about returning to their mountains. "Too bloomin' big Aashvul" was not a comfortable place for them. Neither girl could tolerate all the comings and goings of the numerous and very busy town people. They complained that some folks talked too loud and too much for their peaceful ears to abide. I decided to take their words as a warning for me not to jabber on so.

Lavonia explained that she and Opal had come to work mostly because "kin called fer hep." I knew the kin was Daisy Nell. She must have written for them to come to Asheville after Mrs. McCall talked about how busy my aunt was.

One day close to Christmas, Opal asked to speak with Aunt Mamie. She swallowed and began, "Missres Nash, me and 'Vonie, we's needin'" to be gittin' home soon. But don't ya' worry none about it. We's a'gonna keep our word to ya' and hep long as ya' be needin' us."

My aunt looked sweetly at Opal and called for Lavonia to stop her work to join them.

Mamie knew Daisy Nell made all the decisions for her younger sisters, and she remembered that the young woman had visited with them only a couple days prior. It didn't surprise her to learn that Opal and Lavonia were needed back home. Knowing Opal as I did, it likely took her two days to gather her courage to ask my aunt about leaving.

Aunt Mamie was accepting of the news. "I certainly understand, although it will be difficult to give up such fine assistants as you. I'll go through what is yet to be finished and let you go back to your family as soon as I can."

Opal let go the breath she was holding.

As much as I'd miss Opal and Lavonia, I surely understood the "family" part.

Knowing they wouldn't be with us for much longer, I tried to drink in everything they said. Sometimes Mamie would give me one of her looks. Her lips pinched shut, the frown on her forehead told me not to accept as true everything that was being said. Even so, I believed every word. The story about the bear sitting at their granny's table was my favorite.

"The Lord above can strike me dade with lightin' ifin this ain't the way it wer." Opal raised her hand as if to make a promise and said, "The bar' was a sittin' thar by soup kettle etin' that squirrel meat." She slapped her hand on her lap and shouted, "And that bar' were usin' Granny's fork to et it!"

Aunt Mamie cleared her throat. My guess was it was to keep herself from laughing out loud. Nonetheless, Opal quickly returned to her sewing.

My aunt didn't want Opal or Lavonia to fill my head too full of tall tales. At the same time, she let me know that it was the girls' jobs to concentrate on their sewing, not on entertaining me.

I repeated every story to Elizabeth, and I also wrote the tales to the folks back home. It was my brother Ben, who was twelve, who most enjoyed them. I couldn't write fast enough to satisfy Ben. Knowing him, I expect that by the time he finished repeating the stories to his friends, that bear had eaten a sack full of squirrels and poor Granny along with it.

Since Halloween, Aunt Mamie had worked long into the night and often all by herself. I'd be snug in my bed listening as the rickety-tick of her sewing machine sang me to sleep. One morning as I was gathering my things to walk to school, my aunt mentioned that she'd never had quite so much work to do. She thanked me for doing my part, saying "You have brought the joy of fun and laughter into my all too somber home, Ociee Nash."

I liked that, but I wondered why she didn't brag about my sewing skills. She hugged me, "Oh, dearest, you have come a very long way, and for that improvement, I am most grateful."

I wasn't sure what she meant.

Aunt Mamie also told me she couldn't have accomplished what all she had without Lavonia and Opal. "Bless their dear hearts," she added. My aunt was always blessing folks' hearts.

Every night for the last week, with the exception of Christmas Eve itself, my aunt sent me to bed early. I didn't mind; at least not after Aunt Mamie let me in on the secret of my dress.

Elizabeth helped as Aunt Mamie pinned the hem. "Mind you, dear, keep your eyes closed tightly."

Fortunately, Elizabeth was giving me hints with her "oohs" and "ahs."

"Now take your first look, Ociee."

"*My goodness*," I swooned.

"Ociee, it's the prettiest thing I ever saw," said Elizabeth.

The dress made me think of a Christmas ornament, one big enough for an eleven-year-old girl to crawl inside. It was tea-length silver velvet trimmed with satin cuffs and collar, which were green, the green of a magnolia leaf. A red, green, and silver sash circled my waist. As the best surprise of all, Aunt Mamie cross-stitched "1900" down the left side of the matching shawl.

I threw my arms around her, "Oh thank you, thank you, Aunt Mamie!"

"You are most welcome."

"Elizabeth," began Aunt Mamie, "Your mother Frances tells me you will be wearing your new coat. I made this for you to wear over it." With that, my aunt opened her drawer and brought out a sash embroidered with "1900". The numbers were exactly like those on my outfit.

"See, you can drape it on like so," she said, placing it over my friend's shoulder. "Hook it with this button under your arm."

Elizabeth and I grabbed each other's hands and danced about the sewing room as my aunt applauded. We stopped and applauded her. "Cheers for Aunt Mamie. Cheers for her surprises. Cheers for 1900! Cheers for the brand new century!"

Suddenly, my aunt jerked her head around. She inhaled and exclaimed, "I smell smoke!"

Aunt Mamie and I raced toward the kitchen. Sure enough, smoke was pouring from the oven.

"Stand aside," she cautioned, reaching inside for her cake. "Thank goodness. We got here in the nick of time!"

I turned around, and realizing my friend wasn't there, I hurried back to the sewing room. There stood Elizabeth, statue-still, clutching her sash. Of course, the smell of the smoke frightened her. Ever since the Murphys' home burned down the year before, Elizabeth was absolutely terrified of fire.

"It's all right, Elizabeth. Aunt Mamie's cake almost burned, that's all."

"Is the house on fire?" she quivered.

"No, Elizabeth, it's not."

"Are you sure, there's not fire everywhere?" Tears filled her eyes.

"Yes, I'm certain. Come with me. Aunt Mamie could be cutting us a slice of chocolate cake this very second."

She sniffled.

I urged her down the hallway. Elizabeth hesitated.

"Come on, girl," I encouraged. "I'm hungry. Aren't you?"

Aunt Mamie was loosening the cake from the pan. She looked at Elizabeth and said, "Darling, there's no harm done. You see? The cake was just calling for me to come quickly. It's fine, and you're safe, too. Elizabeth Murphy is as safe as can be."

"Yes, ma'am."

"Ociee, you'd best take off that dress before you muss it. Please do so while the cake is cooling. Elizabeth, will you go with her and make certain she hangs it up properly?"

"Yes, ma'am."

I admired my lovely dress one more time and carefully hung it in the wardrobe. As I adjusted my apron, I noticed that even it had a few spots of whitewash. "Look at this, that paint got everywhere, even inside my coat! But don't concern yourself, Elizabeth, because Aunt Mamie knows how to get stains out."

She didn't respond.

"Oh well, a century turns only once every one hundred years, so a celebration is worth any calamity," I remarked. "Just think, you and I will be one hundred and eleven years old the next time there's a century turning."

She remained quiet.

"Actually, I will be one hundred and eleven, Elizabeth. You'll *only* be one hundred and ten." Even that didn't get a response.

"Aunt Mamie said she might have to insist that her George cooperate with me by wearing his parade hat. Look here. We made one for Mr. Lynch, too. She told him that he must not hurt Ociee's feelings." I swished my apron. "I am sensitive, don't you know?"

"I guess so."

I eyed Old Horse's hat sitting on the bench. I picked it up and put it on again. "I know Old Horse will like this, but I'm not so sure Mr. Lynch will agree to wear his. They match, don't you see? Except that the horse's has places for the ears." With that, I poked my fingers through the holes and wiggled them at her.

Elizabeth smiled a little.

"Look at this," I said showing her the hat. "Mr. Lynch's has a red feather; it's a rooster's tail. Elizabeth, did you know my aunt sometimes calls him 'you old rooster you'?"

"She does?" My friend smiled bigger. "That's so silly!"

A bit miffed at her making fun, I tried to explain, "Mr. Lynch is very confident and proud, just like Hector."

"Hector?"

"Yes, Hector. He was my rooster; he called out to me at daybreak every morning, 'Cock-a-doodle-Ociee.'"

"Wish I had a rooster," sighed Elizabeth.

"Well, I don't have one anymore."

Even though Hector's crowing loud when the sun came up could be an awful sound to a girl burrowed down deep in a warm bed, I surely did long for his cock-a-doodle-dooing once I became a town girl.

Elizabeth interrupted my daydreaming as she confided, "Rooster or not, Mother says your aunt is never going to marry Mr. Lynch."

"Goodness gracious, whatever makes her say such a thing?"

"She told Father that 'Miss Mamie Nash is far too independent a woman to be marrying any man.'"

I shook my head. "Could be. Reckon my aunt is happy enough with Mr. Lynch all the time pleading with her to marry him! Elizabeth, Aunt Mamie told me that his courting made her feel young again. I don't much understand these grown people, do you?"

"I don't. Last week, my mother fussed about something my father did. A few minutes went by, and she walked up and kissed his cheek. I hope we never get old and complicated."

"Let's make a promise about it," I suggested.

We locked our pinkie fingers and squeezed shut our eyes. "We, Ociee Nash and Elizabeth Murphy, promise on this day, December 29, 1899, to stay uncomplicated forever and ever and *ever*!"

"Girls, the cake's ready!"

We raced one another to the kitchen and jumped into the same chair. Almost knocking it over, the two of us leapt up and sat on a second chair. Still together as if we were glued, Elizabeth and I laughed and laughed. My aunt just stood and watched.

"Are you young ladies properly seated yet?"

We separated and sat, "Yes, ma'am!"

Aunt Mamie cut two pieces. The hot chocolate icing dripped from the serving knife. Just watching her, I could all but taste the first bite. Even though the odor of the worrisome smoke still clouded the room, Elizabeth ignored it. The laughter and warm cake had calmed her fear. We gobbled our servings, licked the dripping chocolate from our fingers, and pleaded ardently but very politely for a second helping.

"Here you are," said my aunt. She knew us well and had already sliced two more pieces. "After you two get your fill, young ladies, I want you to go outside and clean up the mess you made."

We grumbled.

"Now, listen to me, my dear girls. Remember, you each made that promise."

"Promise?" I looked at Elizabeth.

"Promise?" she looked at me. We locked pinkie fingers again and started to snicker.

"What is so funny?" asked Aunt Mamie.

"Just promising, that's all!"

I licked the crumbs from the top of my lip.

3

"Has anybody seen my buggy?" shouted George Lynch. "It's missing!"

Elizabeth and I sprang from our seats.

"George, what on earth?" Even my aunt was alarmed.

"I just don't know what to think. I went by the stable for Old Horse and led him over here. I expected to see my old buggy out front, but all I found was a fine carriage. Old Horse is a might confused, too. This new carriage appears to be freshly whitewashed and all decorated with ribbons and greenery."

"*Mister Lynch!*" I squealed, "That *is* your old buggy! Elizabeth and I have been working on it this whole morning long!" I was aglow with my own self-importance.

"No, that can't be mine. It looks to be fine enough for Santa Claus himself to drive. Little ladies, I think Santa accidentally left his buggy parked somewhere on Charlotte Street Christmas Eve night. It must have rolled all the way down the hill to the Nash house."

"Santa doesn't drive a buggy, Mr. Lynch! Besides that, Santa is for little children, not for almost grown girls like Elizabeth and me."

Aunt Mamie chuckled. "I declare, George Lynch, you are a delight. Now, admit it, don't you think that these 'almost grown girls' have worked a wonder with your old carriage?"

"Of course, I do." He sat down at the table to talk with Elizabeth and me. Putting his hands on our shoulders, Mr. Lynch said, "I'd say that you've done a wonderful job. I appreciate how much effort you both have put into this."

I kicked Elizabeth under the table. I didn't like the "both" part much, because I knew I'd done most of the work. Elizabeth kicked me back. As usual, she didn't agree.

Mr. Lynch didn't pay any attention to our kicking. "In fact," he continued, "I don't remember that my buggy looked quite as grand when we got it new. Old Horse and I are so very proud, and we thank you kindly."

"You're welcome." Elizabeth and I grinned at one another. I quickly cupped my hand over my mouth. I had to hold in the pride that was busting out.

My aunt stood at the sink and poured the water she'd been heating into her dishpan. She stirred in chips of old soap to melt. The pans with the burned-on batter would have to soak for a good while. As she slid them into hot soapy water, she turned around. "George, would you like a cup of coffee?"

"Don't mind if I do," he answered eagerly. He eyed the cake. Before I could remember my manners enough to offer him a piece, I thought about my century turning costume. I excused myself and hurried to fetch it. I also grabbed Elizabeth's sash, and as I ran back down the hall with my dress and shawl, and Elizabeth's sash, I got all twisted up in the fabrics. Aunt Mamie had to stop what she was doing and help get me untangled.

"See, this is mine. Aunt Mamie made it especially for me. It's so soft, here, feel it, Mr. Lynch. I love the color, don't you?" I asked but didn't give him the opportunity to answer back.

Elizabeth was straightening out her sash. She wanted to model hers, too.

"And here's the shawl." I stepped close to him. "It'll keep me plenty warm on Monday, don't you think?"

Mr. Lynch grinned. "Warm and very pretty, too."

I blushed. "Thank you, Mr. Lynch. *And*, best of all, look." I indicated my aunt's cross-stitch.

"And mine!" Elizabeth pointed out hers, too.

"So, what do you think, Mr. Lynch?" I finally took a breath.

"With the likes of the two of you, I think all the other neighbors might just as well stay home," he beamed.

We grinned.

"Mr. Lynch, reckon I did forget to ask you a favor." I hesitated. "I, er, well, I sort of promised somebody something without checking with you first."

Elizabeth cut her eyes to me. She mouthed the word, "What?"

I looked at her, and then at Mr. Lynch, and sheepishly pleaded, "Can Elizabeth ride with us, too?"

Aunt Mamie corrected, "Ociee, dearest, that is 'may' ride, not 'can' ride. We know our Elizabeth is 'able' to join you, but you are inquiring as to whether or not Mr. Lynch will invite her to do so."

"May she?"

"May I? Please!" echoed my friend.

"May you, or can you?" he said, looking quizzical. "My answer is 'yes' to both questions. Of course, I was counting on Ociee, and on you, Elizabeth."

I sidled up to Elizabeth and squeezed her hand, but she wasn't ready to squeeze mine back just yet because of the little misunderstanding.

Mr. Lynch continued, "Appears to me that my horse and buggy will be the finest in the entire neighborhood, and we surely will be carrying the most beautifully dressed passengers."

I gave Elizabeth my smug "told you so" look. She tried to be pouty, but she was grinning too much to make a fussy face at me. I always knew Mr. Lynch would let Elizabeth come along. Just the same, I should have asked him before I told her. I was relieved that things worked out all right.

The way Mr. Lynch responded so happy and proud like, I was reminded of Papa and how he glowed any time he was with us children. Mr. Lynch was much like Papa in some ways—that way, for sure.

Now like Elizabeth being compared to me, George was dark-haired and brown-eyed, while George Nash was blond and gray-eyed, like me. However, I had to wonder whether all "Georges" were the same in enthusiasm and caring, and as kind as were George Nash and George Lynch.

"Mr. Lynch," I cleared my throat and smiled hopefully, "have you decided to wear the hat, the one I made to match Old Horse's?"

Aunt Mamie raised her eyebrow at him. He saw her face.

"I don't see why not." He winked at my aunt. For some silly reason, I thought I should wink at Elizabeth. She winked back at me. We were all just winking and blinking like we had gnats in our eyes.

"There is one condition," he added. "I was hoping to carry Miss Mamie along with us. That is, if you'd like to join us. Would you, Mamie?"

Tickling my back, my aunt responded, "I thought I might just ride in one of those modern horseless buggies instead." She grinned slyly.

George Lynch turned beet-red. "Those devil automobiles, a curse to mankind, I say they are. The good Lord gave us horses because He meant for them to pull our buggies!"

My aunt laughed. I wondered if Mr. Lynch was right about God and the buggy pulling.

"Upsetting horses and dirtying up the streets is what they do. And, saints preserve us, all that noise! The other day, I heard one coming from a country mile away," Mr. Lynch's voice grew louder with every word. "They just aren't civilized, I'm telling you the truth about that!"

Mamie patted his back. "Forgive me, my dear George, I shouldn't have teased you."

"Derned loud contraptions!"

"George, dear!"

"I'm sorry, Mamie, but the subject of those demons always riles me up."

Elizabeth whispered to me, "My father is talking about getting one."

I put my finger up to my lips. "Shh, don't be telling Aunt Mamie's beau."

"What, what's that?" asked Mr. Lynch.

"Not a thing, George," answered my aunt. She asked, "How about a big slice of cake? It would taste mighty good with your coffee, too. What do you say, how about another cup?"

"Mamie, are you trying to get my mind off those infernal contraptions?"

"Yes, George, indeed, I am. I have only myself to blame for fanning your fire. I should never have gotten you started."

She put the cake in front of him. He put a fork full in his mouth and fluttered his eyelashes. "Mmm, real tasty, thank you." He paused, "You're right, Miss Mamie, I can't seem to remember what it was that we were talking about."

"Aunt Mamie, I think there's something I'm trying to forget, too. 'May' I have another piece of cake? And please, 'may' Elizabeth also have one?"

"Ociee Nash, although I appreciate that you learned my grammar lesson, my answer remains 'no.' Neither of you may have a third piece. The Murphys would be most unhappy were I to send their Elizabeth home with her stomach full of dessert. Two pieces is a gracious plenty. Run on now and be about your business. As I recall, there are some chores that you promised to do."

"Reckon so," I said. I slipped our plates in the hot soapy water.

"All this conversation about the cake has made me hungry," admitted my aunt. "Mind if I join you, George?"

"Can't think of anything I'd like better."

Elizabeth and I were headed toward the front door, when Mr. Lynch said something that stopped me stone cold in my steps.

"Mamie, with the excitement, I almost forgot that I have something to give you." He stood up, reached into his coat's inside pocket and retrieved an envelope. "It's a letter."

"Why, thank you, George."

"Mr. Hightower at the Post Office had this for you and Ociee, but I told him I'd gladly bring it as I was on my way here. I believe it's a message from Memphis, Tennessee."

"Memphis?" asked my aunt. "Mercy me, maybe it's from our Fred, from Fred Nash."

"Maybe so," he answered as he passed the letter across the table to my aunt's eager fingers.

"Hmm, I'm not certain that I recognize the handwriting to be Fred's," she noted. "Seems different somehow."

I charged back into the kitchen. My heart was jumping around so, it was stuck in the middle of my throat. Elizabeth chased at my heels.

"Aunt Mamie!" I yelled as I stood in the doorway. "What does the letter say? Did Fred have a dreadful accident? Did his train wreck? Oh, Aunt Mamie, is my brother hurt? Is he dead?"

The room was washed in silence.

I could see Fred as clearly as if I were standing right next to him. The train's engine roared in the background like a fiery dragon. I squeezed shut my eyes and could hear its ravenous thunder. There was Fred; and he was working hard, so very hard! He gripped tight his shovel and fed jagged chunks of coal into the locomotive's hungry engine.

There he labored, our tall strong blond-haired Fred. His intense green eyes sparkled in the reflection of the engine's fire. His face was stained dark from the grimy black smoke of the burning coal.

Even so, I could almost hear my Fred whistle in his funny off-key way, just like he used to do when he worked alongside Papa on our farm. As he whistled, was Fred remembering about the farm, about us, about his little sister Ociee? Was he daydreaming about his sweetheart Rebecca?

Fred! Why did he have to leave in the first place? Why did he join the railroad and put himself into this awful danger? Anger burned in me just like the coal in the terrible train's roaring engine.

What was it? What was getting ready to happen to the train, to my beloved brother? Was another train coming toward him from the other direction? If it were, how I hoped Fred didn't know.

Oh, poor, dear Fred. Could he see it coming? If so, was he afraid? If that were so, was Fred crying? Or was he screaming loud over the greedy sound of his train's engine?

No, not my big brother! Fred hardly ever cried.

I would have.

Knowing Fred, he was doing anything he could to stop that train. Likely, he was attempting to help the engineer pull the brakes. If anyone could have stopped the train, my brother would have.

Fred was a hero all right.

I only hoped the hero had time to ask the good Lord to take him straight up to Heaven.

4

My aunt tore open the letter.

I held my breath.

Suddenly her face brightened. Aunt Mamie's mouth dropped open so far I could see her teeth all the way back to behind her tongue.

"It's all right, my darling, the letter *is* from Fred, and the news is good!" She patted the front of her white apron.

Mr. Lynch collapsed in his chair, "Lord have mercy. Ociee girl, you about scared the life out of me!"

"I'm sorry," I whispered hanging my head.

"I must tell you, George, I was thinking the same dark thoughts. Letters have a way of delivering sorrow to folks."

With that, I started to sob.

Aunt Mamie gently sat me down at the kitchen table, caressed my back, and placed the letter in my hand. She then took my chin in her hands, and lifting my face to hers said, "There, there, dear, everything is all right. But, I do think you and I should learn a lesson from this experience. We must try hard not to fear for the worst of things. Now read it, Ociee, for it appears to me that Fred's message is meant more for you than it is for anyone else."

Still trembling, I read as fast as I could, skipping everything but the names of the people who mattered the most. There would be plenty enough time to drink in the details later. The name that jumped off the pages was that of Fred's sweetheart, Rebecca Hutchinson.

"Oh gracious goodness, he's gone and done it, Aunt Mamie!"

Mr. Lynch and Elizabeth leaned forward, while my aunt sat poised with her hands folded on her lap. Only a soft smile indicated her pleasure. A rapid reader, my aunt relished already knowing the news, while I labored to make out my brother's worse than usual scribbles.

Elizabeth's eyes pleaded with me to tell her, but she'd have to wait. First of all, I had to get a hold on my silly self and also get accustomed to Fred's stunning announcement. Mr. Lynch plunged his fork into the cake and ate nearly half the serving in one huge bite.

"No, he hasn't done it yet, but he's gonna. Let's see; oh, here it is: 'On the first Saturday of the month, March 3, 1900, I, Fred Nash will take for my wife, the beautiful Miss Rebecca Hutchinson!' *Wife!*" I threw my hand to my cheek to hold my jaw in place.

"And then, 'Papa gave me Mama's sapphire ring. I gave it to Rebecca two weeks before Christmas.'"

Everyone around my aunt's kitchen table had something cheery to say, everyone but me. I didn't utter a peep.

I laid down the letter and slowly placed my hand on the gold chain that hung around my neck. I ran my fingers down the chain until I came to Mama's locket. I wore her locket always.

In sharing her ring with Fred, Papa had given away yet another piece of Mama. How could he have done such a thing? Papa had actually allowed my brother to give Mama's sapphire ring to somebody who was not even kin to us. I wasn't sure exactly how mad I was, but I knew I wasn't happy. It was going to be mighty hard for me to see that sapphire on any finger but Mama's.

For me, the bright sunshine time for Fred and Rebecca felt more like a rainy day. More and more of my family was breaking into pieces. I tried to stop myself. I wanted to say, "Now, Ociee, be like Papa, be joyful as he always is." I couldn't make me listen, not then anyhow. Papa was always thinking about us children and leaving out any concern for himself. I meant to be more like George Nash than Ociee, but that would take some effort. I read on further.

"Aunt Mamie, Fred wanted me to be the first to receive an official letter about the wedding. He says that it's because I'm the *other* most important girl in his life, next to Rebecca." I sighed. Fred's writing how important I was to him did manage to fluff me up a tad.

"I know dearest, I read that part," said my aunt softly. "You must keep this letter always, Ociee. It will become a most special memento from your older brother. Put it somewhere for safekeeping."

I thought I might paste it in my journal.

The hall clock struck 1 o'clock. "Oh dear!" squealed Elizabeth. "It's way past time for me to go. Ociee, will you come by my house later and tell me what else Fred says? Please?"

I mumbled "yes," but that was about all. I was far too anxious to finish the letter.

Elizabeth gathered up the sash and hurried toward the back door. "I love my sash, Miss Nash, thank you very much!" The door slammed shut behind her as she hollered back, "And thank you for the cake, too, both pieces!"

I didn't say goodbye; I just kept on studying each and every word of the four-page letter in front of me. It was the longest one I'd ever received, even longer than any from Papa.

"More coffee, George?"

"Yes, thank you, Mamie. I'd say congratulations are in order," he commented. "My hat goes off to that young man. I can't seem to make my best girl say she'll marry me."

"Hush, George," chided Aunt Mamie. "Maybe, just maybe I'm saving myself for a railroad man like my nephew."

"Mamie Nash, I'd have another fellow's head if he even thought about courting you," quipped Mr. Lynch. Then he elbowed my aunt. "I know you're just trying to get my goat. Aren't you?"

"That's right, dear."

Pleased, Mr. Lynch took his last bite of his cake and licked the chocolate from his fingers.

I read on. "He has asked Papa to be his 'best man.' What does that mean, Aunt Mamie? Isn't Papa already the very best man Fred knows?"

"You are so right, Ociee. I suppose this is only Fred's way of acknowledging that fact to other people. Actually, darling, the best man has important tasks to perform for the wedding ceremony. In agreeing to do this, George will be in charge of making certain that Fred arrives at the church on time. He also must take care of the wedding ring until the preacher calls for it, and he will have to stand up as one of two witnesses at the church."

"Oh." I didn't much care about what Papa had to do. I did care that everyone in that church would know full well that Papa was better than all the other papas in Mississippi. Best man, best Papa, it was all the same to me. Right then and there I made a decision.

"When I get married I'm going to have Papa be my best man. And Aunt Mamie, will you be my best lady?"

"Yes, my dear, I will."

I shuffled to the last page. "I have a job, too!" I jumped and shouted. When I hopped up, I spilled Mr. Lynch's coffee.

"If you are asked to serve punch at the reception, Ociee, we'd best start our practicing immediately, my darling." Aunt Mamie reached for the linen dishtowel and handed it to me so I could mop up my mess.

"No, I am not to serve punch, but I am to be an attendant. Oh my goodness, Aunt Mamie, what does an attendant do?"

"You, Ociee, are to look pretty and walk down the aisle of the church slowly, gracefully, and with a pleasant smile on your face. Also, you'll carry a lovely bouquet of flowers."

"The 'walking slowly' part worries me some," advised Mr. Lynch.

I blushed and wondered how I'd walk so slow without toppling over backwards.

He continued, "You've been in a hurry since the day I first saw you. Do you remember that buggy ride with me, young lady?"

"Yes, sir! I surely do."

"There you were, nine years old, and full of spit and fire. You ran right over to my carriage. Why you didn't as much as bat an eye when you asked me to carry you to 66 Charlotte Street."

My aunt reached across the table and squeezed tight my right hand.

I thought about what Mr. Lynch had said about me being full of spit and fire. That sounded so funny to me. Seems my spit would put out my fire! I'd have to write to Ben with that funny joke. He'd like that one.

I thought about Aunt Mamie and all that had happened to me since the train trip; new home, different school and friends, Elizabeth, the Murphys' fire, Papa's visit, the farm sold off, now Fred's wedding.

It was hard for me to believe I had spent my second Christmas in Asheville, my second Christmas away from home. Home? Home in Mississippi, or was home forever going to be in North Carolina?

I held tight to Aunt Mamie's hand. She had been like tonic to me. My aunt knew mostly what to say and what not to say, how to listen, and how to hold me close to her in a way that neither one of us needed to whisper a single word to know how we were feeling about something. Aunt Mamie was doing my Mama's job while she was busy singing with the angels. Yet no one, not even my aunt, could take her place. How I needed Mama.

Hard as it was, I had made my aunt happier, too. She said so. I'd helped with the sewing, of course; and I was especially charming with our customers. Aunt Mamie said that, too. I also made her proud with my good grades in school. Like my aunt, I was the best speller in my group. My teacher Miss Small bragged about me in front of her whole class.

I'd also brought George Lynch into our family. Well, not just yet.

Aunt Mamie told me that my coming to live with her turned 66 Charlotte Street near about upside down. At first, she wondered what she had gotten herself into, even though she had pleaded so fiercely with Papa to send me. She also said that now, she couldn't imagine how she had ever gotten along without Miss Ociee Nash by her side.

Now, my aunt never actually admitted that she appreciated my talking her into inviting Mr. Lynch for dinner. She was real quiet about things of that nature. Aunt Mamie mostly made funny things out of her deep down private feelings. So when I asked if she were pleased about Mr. Lynch, she wouldn't say. She only teased, "Ociee, I'm simply relieved that you didn't insisted on seating Old Horse at our dining room table!"

Yet, as much as I liked living in Asheville and so appreciated what Aunt Mamie had done for me, it certainly made my insides flutter to think that in only a few more weeks, I would again be back together with my Papa, my Fred, and my Mississippi. Then it hit me. I leapt from my chair and started to run all around the kitchen screaming, "I can't half believe it! At last, I am going to see my *Ben*!"

5

At exactly eight o'clock on the evening of December 31, 1899, I climbed into my bed to take a four-hour nap. I planned to jump up as soon as the hall clock stuck twelve and run all throughout our house screaming and welcoming the new century.

Pulling the covers up under my chin, I'd twist first one way, then the next. I closed tight my eyes; but as soon as I thought about midnight or about the parade the next afternoon, those eyes of mine would spring wide open.

I spotted my dress hanging on the wardrobe door. The moon's light showed off the "1900." It was as if that moon were saying, "Ociee, get up! It's time."

The hall clock struck nine times. I flipped onto my side so I couldn't see the dress. It worked, and I drifted off to sleep.

The clock chimed one, two, three, four, five, or six, or was it nine or ten? I couldn't remember when I started to count. However, I believed it wasn't close to twelve, so I closed my eyes again. Somehow, my backside made its way out of the covers. Minutes later, I woke up so freezing cold, I thought I was out in the yard. I wrapped up like a sausage in my Mama's quilt.

Sun streamed in through my window. Drat! I'd slept right through the hall clock's chiming and even through all the church bells! I leapt from my bed, and without even bothering to stick my arms in my robe, wrapped it around myself, and raced downstairs.

Aunt Mamie sat at the kitchen table sipping her morning coffee. "I wondered if the *next* century might come around before you arose, 'Sleeping Beauty.'"

"I missed it, Aunt Mamie, I missed the whole thing!"

"Don't worry, darling girl, so did I. However, Mrs. McCall and Daisy Nell filled my ears full!"

Mr. and Mrs. McCall had lived in the house next door for hundreds of years. Between the two of them, they knew just about every person in Asheville. Mr. McCall was a volunteer fireman and a very brave man. In fact, my aunt and I always gave him most of the credit for saving Elizabeth's house when it burned.

After the fire and for several weeks that followed, Mrs. McCall, Aunt Mamie, and I organized the entire neighborhood to come to the Murphys' aid by cleaning, repairing, and storing their things while the house was being rebuilt.

Elizabeth's family had thanked us over and over again. Once they were moved back in, they had a big supper for the folks who had done so much for them during the days following the fire. Mr. Murphy stood up and thanked folks, first the firemen, and second, the friends and neighbors. Then he took a seat and Mrs. Murphy stood and asked for everyone's attention.

I wasn't paying much mind to what she was saying. We were having cherry pie, and I was more concerned about counting my cherries. I was short a few, and Elizabeth was giving me some of hers to equal us out. All of a sudden, her mother singled out my aunt and me. "And very importantly, I want to thank Miss Mamie Nash and her niece Ociee."

Hearing my name had startled me so, I dropped my fork on the floor. I grabbed for it, rose back up and bumped my head on the bottom of the walnut table. Naturally, Elizabeth and I got tickled.

"Ociee, because of you and your Aunt Mamie, Mrs. McCall, and all of our beloved friends in this neighborhood, the Murphy family is once again 'pieced' back together. And, dear child, we are pieced together in such an extraordinary way, I'd like to compare our family's newly rebuilt home to your Mama's so beautifully hand-pieced quilt."

I wasn't giggling anymore. Tears welled up in my eyes and in Aunt Mamie's, too. Mrs. Murphy had talked about Mama and her quilt in front of all those folks. That made me mighty proud. I hoped the Lord told Mama about it, or better, that she heard it for herself.

While I slept that New Year's morning, Aunt Mamie and Mrs. McCall talked over the back fence. Aunt Mamie would recount every detail for me. She must have been about ready to pop just waiting for me to wake up.

"Tell me, oh Aunt Mamie, please tell me everything that Mrs. McCall said. Don't leave out a single thing!"

"Well, dear, it seems that the New Year's Eve celebrations were no more than a bunch of rowdy folks who drank too many spirits and ran wild around our lovely town terrifying the sensible citizens."

"What happened?" I stood wide-eyed.

"Seems some fool hardy soul managed to start a fire over on Spruce in some old abandoned house. It was well after 2 A.M. according to Mrs. McCall. Her poor husband and the volunteer firemen had to get themselves up to go and form a bucket brigade to put out the blaze."

Fire? Crazy folks running around. I knew for certain I'd missed the most exciting night of my whole life.

"Aunt Mamie, go on!"

My aunt shook her head. "Many of the foolish people had pistols and rifles. Ociee, they were running about firing off their guns in the air. It's a wonder that some innocent soul wasn't killed! "

"Guns! Aunt Mamie, I would have loved that!"

"Lord, child, I know," groaned my aunt as she closed her eyes and sighed. "I must remember to say a word of thanks to your guardian angel for making certain that you remained safely asleep! I am most appreciative of your angel's first successful mission of the new year."

"The bells, Aunt Mamie, I missed the church bells!"

"We can hear those grand bells every Sunday morning, my dear. Believe me, it was the best thing that we Nash girls began this century the way we did."

"Drat it all."

"Ociee."

"Yes, ma'am, I know."

I thought about the parade. It was finally going to take place, and on this very day! "What time is it? Has Mr. Lynch come by yet? How many hours until one o'clock?"

"Not to worry, dear, it's early yet. Why, it's not even 8:30. See, you've not slept so late after all. And, no, I've neither spotted George Lynch nor has Old Horse trotted by without him."

"Oh, Aunt Mamie, how silly you are."

"You have at least four hours to prepare yourself, Ociee. That should give you ample time to eat your breakfast, straighten your room, and, I suggest, to say a pleasant 'Good Morning' to me." She made a grumpy face as if she was miffed. I knew she wasn't.

"Oh my goodness, I'm sorry," I kissed her forehead. "Good morning and a Happy New Year to you, Aunt Mamie."

We shared our breakfast of toast and orange marmalade. My aunt made mention that she had waited for me to eat with her. "We must salute the newness of the times by taking this first meal of 1900 together."

We toasted with apple juice. "Here's to you, darling child." We clinked our glasses.

"Here's to you, Aunt Mamie." Again, we clinked the glasses.

For her next turn, my aunt toasted our family. "To George, to Ben, and to our bridegroom Fred and his sweetheart Rebecca." *Clink.*

I was real excited that the wedding would take me back home; but right then, I really wanted to enjoy every minute of what was special about this, the very first day of twentieth century. I did my next toast. "To Mr. Lynch and to Old Horse, and, oh dear! How could I forget, and to Elizabeth." *Clink.* "I'd better not let on that I forgot her until after Old Horse!"

"Let's toast everyone we know," suggested Aunt Mamie. "That way, we'll be certain not to omit anyone. To everyone!" *Clink.*

"To everyone." *Clink.*

After we finished with the meal and the dishes, I got dressed and put on my coat to go outside. Thank goodness it was warming up and there was no rain or snow falling. It looked to me to be the most perfect of days. Our parade would be a grand event; and for Aunt Mamie's sake, there would be no guns firing.

As far as I could see up and down Charlotte Street, people, mostly children like me, were ready to start. I couldn't imagine how any of us would be able to tolerate the waiting. I was so excited that I was about to shake into pieces.

Mrs. McCall had done most of the organizing. Of course, Elizabeth and I had done our parts, and more, to help.

For instance, we copied an announcement over and over on our school tablets and delivered one copy to every house for two whole blocks on both sides of Charlotte Street. We then walked left up Chestnut, where Elizabeth lived, and took the announcements to all of the Murphys' neighbors.

Next, we took another left onto Central doing the same thing; and lastly, we turned left again on Orchard. It took us most of that first week in December to spread the message to all the neighbors on the big square route that Mrs. McCall had designated for our parade.

Come one, come all,
Join your Neighbors' Parade to Welcome 1900!
Marchers, cyclists, horses, baby carriages, buggies,
wagons, children, pets, and grown people may come!

Wear festive clothes and bring musical
instruments, even if you cannot play.
1 p.m., Monday, January 1, 1900
Gather on Charlotte Street
(Between Chestnut and Orchard)

That was how our *best* announcements turned out. After we'd written ten of them, they weren't all quite as neatly done. Some were missing words. I had ink in my hair and all over my fingers. So did Elizabeth. But since her hair was black, the ink only showed on her hands and face.

I scratched my nose twice and accidentally made a big black mustache. Elizabeth laughed so hard I ran up on the porch to see my reflection in the window. The mustache looked real funny so I added a beard! Elizabeth made glasses and a handlebar mustache on her face.

"Goodness, girl, you look just like your father. I'm gonna call you Mr. Murphy 'til you get washed!"

"All right then, *Mr. Hightower*! You look enough like him that you could take over his job at the Post Office!"

Elizabeth and I always got along fine, that was, until we disagreed about something. The "musical instruments" on our announcements became one such issue. I knew the more noise we had, the better the parade would be. That included folks banging pots and pans. Elizabeth insisted that only talented people with actual instruments be encouraged to play. Neither of us was about to bend.

I recalled to her about how Papa always enjoyed his harmonica. "And so did we. It didn't matter if he played well or not. To Ben and me, it was all the more fun when he hit a wrong note." I smiled at the funny memory.

"Yes, but he was playing for you, Ociee. This is for a big parade!"

If my friend were going to give in, it would take some powerful convincing from me; and she was too set on her own opinion to listen. Elizabeth even wanted to have her own piano in the parade.

"Your piano!"

"No, not really, I just wish I could play is all," she admitted.

"You can carry a pot and metal spoon like me."

Elizabeth answered with an ugly face. Fact was, she *still* hadn't decided what to do about making her own music; and there it was, the day of the parade. Elizabeth could be so stubborn.

It wasn't long before I spotted Mr. Lynch's buggy coming up our street. I could recognize Old Horse's trot even when I was facing the opposite direction and couldn't see him. First there was a steady clop, clop, clop, then a pause, and a clop, clop. That horse always trotted faster once he spotted me!

He would stop, stand straight, and point his hoof in the manner of a graceful dancer. That right hoof was the only graceful feature about Mr. Lynch's horse. Old Horse was a tall and massively built chestnut horse with great heavy legs. His golden lashes framed his eyes and made him look as though he were wearing grandfather glasses.

"Happy nineteen hundred, Mr. Lynch." I ran to greet him.

"A most happy New Year's Day to you, Miss Ociee."

"*And* to you, Old Horse." I walked to the front of the buggy to pat his nose. "No sir, sorry, but I don't have a carrot for you this morning. You best be patient and you may get a surprise."

Old Horse reared his head, snorting out air that I could see because of the cold. His jowls flared and steam circled his nose.

"The carriage looks absolutely elegant this morning, don't you think, Mr. Lynch?"

"Yes, indeed, young lady. Don't you know that since you girls finished it on Friday, my passengers have had many nice things to say! Perhaps it's good for business."

"We'll decorate again for Valentine's Day!"

Mr. Lynch nodded, biting his lips. I was certain that meant he liked the idea.

I started to fiddle with the holly and the bows, but Mr. Lynch called for my attention. "Ociee, I think my horse expects something. See how he's rearing his head? That horse is trying to talk with you."

"His usual carrot is what he wants, Mr. Lynch. But look here, I have something even better for him."

I unbuttoned my coat and opened my apron pocket. Inside was a half-cup of sugar wrapped in a hankie. I emptied it into my hand and held it out for him to lick. The horse's tongue tickled my fingers. I couldn't help it; I had to wiggle. Old Horse kept right on licking with his big pink tongue.

When he was done, I wiped my hands on my apron. That horse didn't let out the first whinny to say "thank you." All he cared about was the taste of the sugar. "That's all right, boy, I know you enjoyed your treat. Now I must insist you return the favor." I ran up to the porch to get the top hats off the swing.

With one in each hand, I hurried back.

"I just don't know how Old Horse is going to react to wearing a hat," worried Mr. Lynch, "but let me help you get it on."

"Please put yours on first," I pleaded. "If he sees yours, he may get the idea and like his better." It was fairly apparent that neither our friend nor his horse was taken with the top hats. Nevertheless, Mr. Lynch placed his on his head and grinned real big acting happy as could be.

"Old Horse, I must appear as quite a sight in this hat! Now, how about we see yours on you?" whispered Mr. Lynch, as he gently adjusted the catch under the wary horse's chin.

Old Horse shook his head back and forth. The hat stayed put.

"Easy boy, easy," soothed Mr. Lynch.

"Good boy," I beamed.

Elizabeth and her father rounded the corner about the time the horse settled into wearing the top hat.

Elizabeth ran toward us as Mr. Murphy, hurrying to catch up, burst into a big smile. "I'll be, George Lynch, but if you and your fine steed don't look like a couple of brothers!"

Elizabeth and I got real tickled.

Mr. Lynch muttered something back at Elizabeth's father, but we couldn't understand, because we were laughing so loud.

Aunt Mamie walked from the porch, shivering. She pulled her shawl tight around her shoulders, tucking her hands inside. "Sounds as if I might be missing some fun. I like your hat, George."

Mr. Lynch tipped it toward her. "Good morning, Miss Mamie, and a Happy New Century to you."

"And to you, dear sir." She spotted Old Horse and snickered. "I just have to wonder how my father would feel about a horse trotting down Charlotte Street sporting his hat!"

I said, "If he's anything like Papa, he'd laugh about it."

"Well, because your Papa is our father made over, I figure our father must be looking down chuckling along with all of us."

I liked knowing that. I'd never gotten to meet my grandfather because he died before I was born. I especially liked that Papa was him all over again, so's now I could think about the both of them. I'd surely make a note of that in my journal. I must remember to share what she said with Ben and Fred, too.

I checked again with Mr. Lynch. He assured me that he and Old Horse were fine about wearing the hats. I suggested that they take them off for the time being. Old Horse looked at me as if to say, "Thank you, Ociee, for the reprieve."

By 12:30, the neighbors began to gather. All us children were excited and nervous and almost hot, even though the day was fairly chilly. We were running about in circles and squealing, and Elizabeth and I were showing off the special clothing my aunt had made for us. She and I were the only participants I noticed with specially sewn New Year's outfits with "1900." Aunt Mamie stood on the front steps watching. I twirled around holding wide the skirt of my velvet dress.

Mrs. McCall announced that it was time to begin lining up everyone. Elizabeth and I ran over to her and asked if Mr. Lynch's buggy could be in the lead.

"Girls, I think not," she answered. "Should Old Horse happen to go to the bathroom, our marchers would step in the, well, you understand, dears, in the excrement."

Excrement was a big word, but I understood exactly what it meant. Back on our farm, I used to step in Maud's excrement every time I went to the pasture. I called it "horse mess." We agreed with Mrs. McCall, and so did everyone else. Of course, most folks knew how to avoid such; but being in a grand parade might make some forget to look out for it. The buggies and the horses with riders would definitely plan to stay to the back.

The smallest children were ushered to the front of the group. Accompanied by their flag-waving, gaily-garbed parents, the little ones were dressed in their best winter clothes. Older children jumped in behind them as everyone began to dance and make merry. Our flyers had made a difference, too, because many people were playing tinhorns, drums, and even pie pans. There were so many American flags; it looked like the 4th of July!

A war veteran tooted his bugle and awakened a sleeping hound on Mr. White's porch. His dog started to howl. To Elizabeth and me, his howling sounded like he was singing.

A girl named Annie, our friend from Orchard Street, dressed her kittens as babies and placed them in her infant sister's carriage. It was a clever idea until one of her kittens jumped out and scampered up an oak tree across the street. Two big yellow dogs took off after the kitten and tried to climb the tree after the frightened animal. The dogs barked and barked. Some boys attempted to call them back into the line, but then they started to argue and got into a fistfight. They got to kicking and hitting and their parents had to pull them apart.

"Oh my, I'd better get our parade started, before we lose our participants," said Mrs. McCall. She rang her porch bell. DING-DONG, DING-DONG!

Mr. McCall shouted as loud as he possibly could, "Attention, ladies, gentlemen, and children, and horses, dogs, and cats!" He laughed. "And that includes the kitten up in the Wallaces' tree! Please, may we have your attention!" He took a deep breath and bellowed, "Now, everyone, let our 'Turn of the Century Parade' *begin!*"

Off we went, short one kitten, two yellow dogs, and two boys whose mothers were pinching them by their ears as they walked home. Sitting there in the front of the buggy beside Mr. Lynch, I was shaking right down to my toes. Too excited to utter a word, I squeezed Elizabeth's hand. It was a grand and glorious event as Charlotte Street began to throb with the pound of marching feet.

"Elizabeth, you forgot your noisemaker!"

"No, I didn't," she said, and started to squeal.

I pitched my pot and spoon down in the grass and squealed along with my very best friend.

Ladies and men strutted arm in arm, parents held their children's hands; some pushed carriages over the street's bumpy bricks, and others pulled wagons filled with little ones holding their pets. Dogs of all kinds ran in and out among the people, who began to stride and wave to folks who were lining the street, standing in their yards, or sitting on front porches. People waved back; some had flags and banners. Babies yelped. The sun shone brightly, bouncing light off the musical instruments and off the pots and pans. Seeing that, I jumped down off the buggy and retrieved mine. "If you change your mind, Elizabeth, I'll share!"

We actually had a band of sorts. Like our firefighters, the band was made up of volunteers. First to pass were three young girls, who must have been visiting because Elizabeth and I didn't have the slightest idea who they could be. Dressed in brown rabbit coats, they were playing silver triangles. Elizabeth pointed to them and said, "They make me think of dancing bears!"

Two boys followed them. One named Oliver was turning cartwheels; the other, Tucker, played a harmonica. I heard the harmonica and wondered what my Papa was doing right then. As much as I didn't want to admit it, Tucker played better than Papa did. What I wouldn't have given to see Papa come marching along.

The band also included two drummers in mismatched outfits, one red, another faded blue. Several members of the North Carolina War Veterans followed a horn player who marched proudly in his Confederate uniform. Two of those men also beat drums; several blew bugles, while one played a piccolo.

Other veterans followed, escorting ladies from the Robert E. Lee chapter of the United Daughters of the Confederacy. They wore their ribbons of honor. I recognized some of the ladies as Aunt Mamie's customers because they had on beautiful garments she'd made for them. The ladies waved to my aunt, who returned their greetings. Aunt Mamie decided to remain on the porch so she could report to us from that vantage point. As I watched her, I told Mr. Lynch that she reminded me of a queen who was waving to her royal subjects.

He replied, "Our Mamie is a queen!"

"Oh, Mr. Lynch, I'm going to tell her you said so."

"Fine with me."

We continued to wait for Mr. McCall's signal for us to start. Elizabeth and I were both getting impatient. "Any minute now, girls," encouraged Mr. Lynch. "Whoa, boy," he called. "I 'spect this horse is feeling just as excited as the two of you."

"Old Horse is near about to pop then!" I said, again getting to my feet to look around at everybody.

"Elizabeth, can you stand it!"

"Not hardly, Ociee, not hardly at all!"

Last in line behind the marchers was a fellow in a fancy gold-colored uniform that even Mr. Lynch didn't recognize. The man played a shiny set of brass cymbals so loud that we had to hold our ears. I told Elizabeth I thought he must have been a real honest-to-goodness musician. I whispered, "Do you think he is from way up north somewhere, maybe even Europe?"

"Europe's my guess," she said.

"And, imagine, he came to Asheville for our parade!"

Next came people riding horses. The men were dressed real fancy with tall hats like the ones Mr. Lynch and Old Horse were wearing. But what got my attention were the ladies who rode sidesaddle. The long flowing skirts they wore covered up the entire horse. At that point Old Horse was fidgeting because of his hat; I had to wonder how in the world those ladies' horses could tolerate wearing a dress. I also tried to imagine how the farmers in Mississippi would take to seeing their girls sitting sideways on a horse. Seemed pretty foolhardy to me. A person might fall off!

The most unusual animal in the parade wasn't a horse or a dog or a cat or even our Old Horse in grandfather Nash's silk hat. It was an opossum! I'd seen him from time to time outside the City Hall at the east end of Pack Square. The opossum belonged to an apple merchant. To attract folks' attention, the merchant often had him hanging upside down from the rung on the front of his covered wagon. Mr. Lynch knew who the apple man was, and somehow he managed to convince the fellow to join our parade.

At long last, it was our turn to go. We fell in about six carriages behind the apple man. I could see the opossum swinging back and forth. "Elizabeth, reckon if that poor thing is getting dizzy?"

"Hope he doesn't upchuck like I did on the train!"

"Yucky!" we both screamed.

Old Horse started to move. We quickly forgot about the opossum and began to beat on my pot. I started to scold Elizabeth, saying she should have brought her own pot or pan, but the day was too happy for me to be fussy.

About then, Mr. Lynch said, "Whoa, whoa, Old Horse. What do you girls say we be the last ones? That way, we'll not show up anybody?"

I agreed, but I was somewhat reluctant. What I'd planned was for our position to be right up in front of the other buggies, so's to make ours look the most important. Naturally, I was thinking about that fancy Mr. Vanderbilt.

The reason the Vanderbilts weren't invited to participate with us that day was because they didn't live in our neighborhood. We weren't being snooty; we had to stick to the rules.

Mr. Lynch was most relieved that no horseless carriage had dared to show up. He even remarked, "Old Horse is nervous enough with all this commotion without having to dodge those demons! You ladies ready?"

"Yes, sir!" we squealed.

He clicked his tongue, "Giddy up, Old Horse!"

Elizabeth and I about burst with joy. "Oh, Mr. Lynch, it is all so perfect! Don't you think?"

He was too busy waving at Aunt Mamie to answer.

As we turned onto Chestnut Street, I could see all the way to the front of our parade. My heart swelled so in my throat, I near about cried. Our parade was an entire block long! Nobody's wedding, not even Fred's, could ever be as thrilling as that event was for me. Old Horse might have felt differently because of the hat. Now our buggy, that was another story all together. Our buggy was the best of all. No one else's even came close.

6

As I looked back on the last few weeks, I felt like I'd been riding on the tiptop of a big old tornado. It was a happy tornado, if there were such a thing, one made from white sugar and soft squishy cotton and carried atop swirling angels' wings.

We'd celebrated Thanksgiving with the McCalls and had so many tasty dishes I didn't make the effort to list them all in my journal. My favorites were candied sweet potatoes, spice cookies, apple cake, and chess pie. Mrs. McCall said, "Ociee, little wonder you're so sweet, everything you enjoy is made from sugar."

At Christmastime, Aunt Mamie and I decorated our house using festive bow ribbon and fresh-cut greenery from our yard. Mr. Lynch took me to select the biggest Christmas tree I'd ever had, and he cut it down with help from me. New Year's brought our big parade; and before we got over that, it was Valentine's Day. Elizabeth and I put red paper hearts all over Mr. Lynch's buggy. He said, "I declare, you two girls are about as clever at attracting customers as that apple farmer friend with his ugly opossum!"

Elizabeth said, "I know, we could tie Miss Kitty Cat to your buggy!"

"If Aunt Mamie gets wind of your idea," I warned, "she will hang *you* upside down!"

Just three days later, there I was sitting on the train making my way back home. To think, tomorrow I'd be at the Abbeville depot! My stomach flip-flopped. I was so excited that I couldn't swallow my own spit.

When Fred, Ben, and I were real little, we had white blond hair just like Papa's. He sometimes referred to us three as "my darlin' kernels" or "my beloved corn on the cob."

Mama did not appreciate his jest in the least. "Kernels of corn, indeed!" She shook her finger saying, "George Nash, your pet names for our extraordinary children make them sound ordinary."

"How about 'golden nuggets' then?"

"You'd best hush your mouth, my dear," she teased, "I'm about to forget why I love you so."

I couldn't tell whether remembering things of that sort made me feel better or made me feel worse. Worse, I decided. I sank down into the seat and started to be sorry for myself.

Then, just as suddenly, I sat straight up and realized that in twenty-four hours, Papa's arms and Ben's arms and Fred's, and mine, too, would be wrapped around one another. My heart whirled around fast as an acorn in a waterspout.

I hadn't seen Ben or Fred since early morning on September 1, 1898. That was way too long for a girl to be away from her brothers. Fred, who was nearly eighteen then, was more like a grown person than he was a brother. To my way of thinking, he couldn't have been as sad as Ben. Oh, my poor Ben! He was ten years old when I left, and we'd always had one another for company. I reckon he'd had as hard a time as me being apart like that. I missed Ben something terrible.

Like all brothers, Ben made me awful mad sometimes. One thing he'd do was to insist he could run faster than me. He was telling a tale about that. I could outrun him anytime I put my mind to it. Even so, during those long months away from him, I would have been happy to have Ben's boasting back, if only for one day.

Most of what I recalled about Ben that last morning, that sad last morning together, were the tears rolling down his cheeks. Tears were rolling down his Ociee's cheeks, too.

"Be careful, my darling child!" The wind whipped her skirt as Aunt Mamie huddled closer to Mr. Lynch and waved her hankie at me. It was a cold February day. My aunt's tears were streaming, too. Us Nashes tended to cry when we had to say good-bye to one another.

"I'll miss you, Aunt Mamie!" I tried to yell over the train's shrill whistle. I was hanging out the window so far I almost tumbled back out onto the platform. Not yet onboard the train for a full minute, and I'd already messed up my hair when I took off my traveling hat. My aunt had worked hard to arrange it to stay. I'd have to be more careful with my dress; it was my favorite calico. Its deep blue shawl perfectly matched the tiny cornflower design.

"Good-bye, Miss Ociee," shouted Mr. Lynch. I could still hear his deep voice calling out to me.

Poof! Asheville was gone. I was astounded. Way back those long months ago when we pulled out of the depot in Abbeville, my hometown had faded very slowly into the train's thick black smoke. Asheville disappeared the minute we rounded the first bend.

I settled into my seat. I'd grown so much since my last trip! I noticed that right away, because of the way the seat fit me. It didn't allow nearly as much room as before. However, I also noticed that the scratchiness of the seat felt exactly the same. Its velvet cover wasn't soft like the velvet of my parade dress.

Strange that Papa hadn't fussed any about his seat when he came to visit last spring. Perhaps people's papas aren't as sensitive to itchy things as their daughters are. *Daughter.* I was certainly old enough to be considered *a daughter*, but Papa kept on telling people that Ociee was his "baby girl." I didn't much like that.

I was hoping I was as close to grown as Ben, but I wasn't counting on it. Papa wrote me that Ben was almost as tall as Fred.

Your brother, at age twelve, still has twice as much energy as a wild colt. That boy eats like a full sized pig, but runs around so much he whittles himself down to skinny as a stick. Ben will make you think about an old scarecrow blowing around in the cornfield.

I'd soon see for myself. I glanced out the window. The smoke was blowing back over the top of our train, making the view ahead quite clear. My goodness, were the Blue Ridge Mountains getting smaller? "Don't be silly, Ociee," I scolded myself. "You've been around those mountains for such a long time that you're starting to take for granted how big they are."

I knew I wouldn't be able to locate Opal and Lavonia's cabin. They told me that. "Lord goodness, girl, even ifin you was on foot and knew 'xactly where to look, you'd still have a time gettin' thar."

Still, I expectantly gazed out into the bluish-gray mountain peaks for sight of the girls. Fresh dabs of winter white glistened in the sun. I wanted to believe it was them sending messages to me with slivers of mirrored glass.

I thought about Opal and Lavonia. How different from me they were, yet how much we were the same. Like me, they were happy enough in Asheville; yet like me, they yearned for a family in another place.

Aunt Mamie had given them extra pay just before Christmas as she thanked them for their wonderful help. "I know you need to return home, my dears. We also want you safely there before the hard snows cover the mountains. Ociee and I would worry," she explained.

"Thanky kindly, Missres Nash," said Lavonia. "Opal and me, we's grown attached to you and to Ociee 'specially." She hugged me, and I could tell she was sniffling some.

Opal spoke up, "We'd be awillin' to come back." She winked her brown eye at my aunt. "Ya just be atellin' Daisy Nell, if ya take a mind to it."

"I'll count on that, my dear."

"Me, too. I love your stories!"

"Them stories, they's jist life, little darlin'."

Home. Like Opal and Lavonia, I was going home, too.

Would it seem different to me?

I clutched my fingers into fists when I remembered that our home was gone! My head kept reminding me, but my heart turned away from the reality that Papa had to sell our farm. He'd come all the way to Asheville to tell us, to tell me.

There would be no familiar house, no barn, no flowers that Mama tended, no fields that Papa and Fred planted season after season. There'd be no water well, no Hector the rooster, no Maud the horse.

There'd be no Gray Dog.

My stomach jerked in a knot. Our family's wonderful Gray Dog ran off just as Papa and Fred loaded the last piece of furniture onto the wagon. A few days later Papa found him. Gray Dog was dead. When Papa told me what happened, I about cried my eyes out. I believed Gray Dog died rather than give up his home.

Even my calf Rebecca was sold.

"Lord," I prayed, "Don't let Rebecca's new owner eat her."

Rebecca. I'd named my calf after Fred's sweetheart, but she never did understand the honor of it. Now my calf was gone and Fred was fixing to marry her namesake. I knew that people were more important than cows; but for the life of me, that was hard to accept.

The mountains grew still smaller.

When Aunt Mamie told me she had decided to stay in Asheville and miss Fred's wedding, I cried. I wanted to have our whole family together again. Truth was, I didn't merely cry when she told me; I pitched an all out "Ociee fit." I hadn't had one of those in a mighty long while. Afterwards, I went out on our front porch and sulked. After a good long time, Aunt Mamie came outside to talk to me.

"Ociee, I know why you want me to travel with you."

I was still fuming. "No, you don't, Aunt Mamie. It is *not* because I'm scared. I came all this way by myself. You remember."

"Yes, of course, I remember," she tried to continue, but I interrupted.

"And it's not because I want to show off to let you see how smart I am about traveling either!"

"Ociee, I know. You are a very smart girl and even more grown up now than you were then."

"That's right, Aunt Mamie. It's, it's—well, I only wish that all us Nashes could be together in one place. You, me, Papa, Fred, Ben. Please, can't you change your mind? We can go purchase you a ticket this very minute. Oh please," my voice trailed off as I started to cry again.

Aunt Mamie snuggled next to me on the porch swing and whispered, "You want me to come along because you love me, dearest. That's more important to me than you will ever know."

My answer was a sniffle.

"But, Ociee, I simply cannot make this journey with you. Something is just holding on to me; something I can't explain is keeping me here. Also, I have my work. Most importantly, however, you need to have these few weeks with George and your brothers. I know this time will be one of making memories. Please, dear, try to understand."

I listened and sniffed again.

"Besides, if I went with you, there would be no aunt waiting to welcome you back to Asheville. How much nicer for you to return and have *this* home waiting for you, just like it was when you were nine years old."

I rubbed my eyes. "With a 'Welcome Ociee to Asheville' feast?"

"Yes, dear," she affirmed. "That's a promise. And I will meet you at the train station, too."

"Or I will signal for Mr. Lynch's buggy. He and Old Horse will get me home fast as lightening. He sometimes drives fast, but he drives good, too."

"Drives *well*, dear, he drives well," she corrected.

"So, well and fast, too!" I jumped out of the swing, kissed my aunt, and skipped into the house.

I opened the basket that Aunt Mamie had packed for me. She'd included a holly branch with a bunch of red berries. I knew not to eat the berries; they were there only to remind me of our yard. The basket was filled with some of my favorite things to eat: a leftover biscuit from our breakfast with my favorite orange marmalade, a banana, two sandwiches, and powder sugar cookies topped with roasted pecans.

As I fingered through I spotted something under one of the sliced chicken sandwiches. It was a note. I figured it was from Aunt Mamie, but I was wrong. It was from Elizabeth.

My Dear Friend Ociee,

Don't you be thinking about staying in Mississippi. Mississippi. I wrote it twice because Mississippi—3 times!—is the longest word I ever wrote. Please do not stay there forever, because I could not bear it. Bear? Are there bears out west in Mississippi? Ociee, do you remember the cubby dancing bears in our parade, the ones who were really girls?

Mother and Father said they would keep me busy the month you are away, but they are not nearly as much fun as you. DO NOT TELL THEM. I even miss the hard work you always make me do on Mr. Lynch's buggy.

There is something else I have learned, Ociee. It is easier to be the person who travels somewhere than it is to be the person who is left behind. I am sorry Mother and I had to be in Georgia such a long, long, long time after our fire. I can now see how sad you were, because you are not leaving me until tomorrow, and I already miss you today.

I do hope you have fun with Ben. I hope you will bring him to meet us.

Your best friend ever, do not forget,
Love,
Elizabeth

P.S. If there are bears in Mississippi, do not get near one of them because they might eat you.

I read Elizabeth's letter ten times while I ate my picnic. I was going to miss my friend. I tasted one of the cookies. I would miss Aunt Mamie's cookies, too.

It seemed to me that my mountains were sinking. It was as if they were melting into the ground like my snow houses once the sun came out. I looked at the Blue Ridge Mountains for a long time knowing I'd soon be homesick for them. I squeezed my eyes tight, like Papa taught me, and made a picture inside my head.

Gracious, but I was a hard girl to please. When I was in Asheville, I was lonesome for Mississippi. Finally on my way to Mississippi, I was already pining for the mountains, for Elizabeth, and for Aunt Mamie's cookies. I looked for somebody to talk to before I went plum crazy.

7

I talked to a couple of folks. The one I liked especially was a boy who got on at the first stop. He had red hair, the brightest red hair I'd ever seen and more freckles than seemed his face could hold. His name was Horace; he was three years older than me. I gave him one of my cookies. After he ate it, he didn't care much about talking; but I kept after him anyway.

Horace told me he had to get off in three more stops and that he was going to visit his grandmother. I found out that Horace would be staying with her longer than I was to be with Papa and my brothers.

"My Maw's got real sick," he explained, "so Paw is sending me to Grannie. My brother Earl is going to our cousins."

I felt awful for the boy. "Hope your mother will get well. What I mean is, I hope she'll get well real soon."

"Yep." Horace leaned forward and looked around me out the window.

I gave him a second cookie.

He ate it, but forgot to say thank you. I didn't mind. Sometimes boys don't remember their manners, especially when they're worried. I offered him another cookie, and he gobbled it down.

He wiped his mouth on his shirtsleeve. "You fix these?"

"I know how, of course, but my Aunt Mamie baked these for my trip. I'm going all the way to Mississippi. Matter of fact, I'll have to change trains in Chattanooga. The terminal there is the biggest place you could ever imagine but I'm not nervous." That was a bold-faced Ociee fib.

Horace replied, "My grannie cooks good, too." Seemed he wasn't much interested in hearing about me or mine. "I 'spect my grannie'll have somethin' tasty waitin' for me when I get to her house."

"'Spect so. Then you won't be wanting any more of my cookies?" I'd already shared more than a fair amount.

"I didn't say that! Say, what's your name?"

"Ociee, Ociee Nash."

"Ociee Ociee?"

"No!" I giggled. "Just one Ociee!"

He laughed, too.

Horace and I got into a discussion about whose aunt or grandmother was the best baker. In the end, neither one of us would budge; so I decided to mention that my aunt was also a seamstress and that she was teaching me how to be one, too.

He puffed up and said, "Grannie makes clothes for near about every person in our family. She even made my paw his Sunday suit!"

I smirked. "Aunt Mamie and I sew for customers! Lots of customers, real fine ones. They pay us money for the things we make for them. All the fanciest ladies in Asheville want to wear our hats and dresses."

With that I'd won.

The train slowed to stop.

"Here's where I get off." Horace all but smashed me flat looking for his grandmother. "There, there she is!" As the train pulled into the depot, he gathered up his things. "Ociee, I liked talkin' with you. It made the trip go fast for me." He stood up, shuffled his feet, and added, "You helped me quit thinkin' about my maw some. Thank you kindly for them cookies, too. They was mighty good."

"You're welcome, Horace. Hope your mama's gonna feel better."

Other folks got off with him and several new passengers got on. As we pulled out of the station, I saw Horace in his grandmother's arms. Even though the old lady was part gray-haired, I could tell the boy had gotten his red from her. I sure did hope his mama didn't have the measles.

There were still a few mountains around us, little ones anyways. I noticed a well-dressed lady who was seated right across the aisle. I wished I hadn't given so many cookies to Horace, because the lady was real skinny and I figured she must have wanted something to eat. I offered her just one.

"No, little girl, no thank you," she answered. "You see I am watching my figure."

There wasn't much figure to watch. She was so bony that her hat was loose and wobbled on the top of her head whenever she talked.

The most interesting thing about the lady was her needlework. She was working on small crocheted circles. They were different pastel colors, mostly pinks and yellows.

"I call them my little whatnots," she explained. "They look rather attractive on a lady's dresser, you see, under her perfumes and such. I use them as gifts when I am a guest in someone's home."

I was accustomed to Aunt Mamie's teaching me to do things, so I asked her to show me how.

"Oh no, that wouldn't be at all possible!" she snapped, stuffing every strand of thread in a cloth bag.

My mouth dropped wide open. I couldn't think of what I should say back to her. That bony lady had hurt my feelings! The idea that she would absolutely refuse to teach me to make her dumb whatnots made me turn red in the face.

The day Aunt Mamie taught me the word "cordial," I included it in a sentence in my journal. I reached into my traveling bag and referred back to that entry. *When a person travels, she should try to act cordial.* I decided to give the lady another try. I began by apologizing for failing to introduce myself before offering her the cookie. "My aunt is teaching me about being a lady."

She replied, "Nice of her."

"I'm sorry, I should have told you my name. I am Ociee Nash. I'm from Asheville and from Abbeville, too. Asheville is in North Carolina and Abbeville is in Mississippi."

She told me her name was Penelope. Not only did she not tell me her last name, but she also would not say where she lived! Maybe she was jealous because she only lived in one place not two like me. Or perhaps she was a famous villain fleeing a dreadful crime. I wished for Elizabeth. Together, she and I could figure things out.

My curiosity was growing, so I asked Penelope another question. "Ma'am, do your friends call you Penny?"

The lady all but collapsed. Her hat began to vibrate and she squeaked, "Penny! Heavens above, no they don't, you persistent child!"

I didn't know the word "persistent." I'd ask Papa. But judging from the tone of her voice, it wasn't a compliment. Maybe I wouldn't find out the meaning because it might make me feel bad. I did try to spell it out in my book. "P-u-r-r," maybe it had something to do with cats, "s-i-s-t-a-n-t." Penelope could not have had very many friends.

The last thing I shared with her was that I was on my way to my brother's wedding. I also mentioned that I'd named my calf Rebecca for my sister-to-be. I added, "That's Rebecca, not 'Becky.'"

Penelope didn't respond. I figured the poor thing either fainted from hunger or drifted off to sleep.

I decided to take a nap, too. I'd tossed about so much the night before I was getting drowsy. Big things like train trips make a person's body too excited to let its eyes shut. I had the very same problem on New Year's Eve, and, as I recalled, the last time I traveled. My eyes were worn out so they rested easily behind my lashes.

Somebody bumped my arm and I woke up. My head was so filled with cobwebs that a spider might well have crawled out my ear. When I turned in my seat and looked outside, I realized it was already starting to get dark. Granted, winter days didn't last very long, but I surely didn't intend to sleep most of that one away. Land sakes, with my talking and eating and sleeping, I'd missed out on what was left of North Carolina and much of Tennessee!

I asked the conductor how much longer before Chattanooga.

"Young lady, we'll be there in under an hour."

I quickly gathered my things. Aunt Mamie allowed me to use her traveling bag, saying that was another good thing about her not coming. For me it was like having a piece of her at my side. She and I carefully packed three play outfits, my dungarees, my journal, two schoolbooks, my brushes and bows, my under things, of course, my nightgowns, the tiny painting of Mama, and, most important, my dress for the wedding.

The week after Fred's letter came to tell us the news, Rebecca's note arrived to invite me, officially, to be her attendant. My aunt told me I was very fortunate to have such a polite sister-in-law. I didn't say much because I wasn't real happy about having a sister, "in-law" or otherwise. I liked being the only girl in the Nash family.

"Only girl?" responded my aunt, "And what does that make me? Don't forget, I am a Nash, and a girl, I'd like to remind you!"

"Aunt Mamie, you're not a girl. You're a lady."

My aunt made one of her faces like she was offended, but she understood exactly what I meant.

She advised me, "However you feel, Miss Nash, you'd better be getting used to the idea of having a sister. Nothing is apt to change about that."

I frowned.

"Come on," she smiled, "let's get busy designing something beautiful for you to wear. We 'girls' like pretty dresses, you do understand. The right dress can make us feel better about even our more difficult situations."

"All right, Aunt Mamie." I sighed and read the rest of Rebecca's letter out loud. "It says I must wear a long dress and it can be made from any shade of pink I choose."

"I know just the color," offered my aunt.

"I choose red. Red is a dark pink."

"Indeed, *not*," she retorted.

"Let's see," I read on, "Rebecca writes, 'With your peaches and cream complexion and pretty blond curls, I think you will look perfectly lovely in pink.' Aunt Mamie, I like what she said about my complexion."

"Perhaps Rebecca won't be so dreadful, after all, Ociee?"

"Maybe not," I grinned without letting her see.

My dress, according to Aunt Mamie, should be feminine, but not too frilly. I agreed with her. If I'd had one of those girlish gowns, Ben would tease me so I'd have to hit him. I was determined to act like the lady I'd practiced being. Something inside of me wanted to show off for the folks back home. Papa would appreciate that. After all, he'd sent me to Aunt Mamie's home to become a lady. I wanted him to see that I was on my way.

"I'm sewing so fast," said my aunt, "the foot pump on my machine will need extra oil!" In the end, my dress was worth her effort, and worth all the oil, too. The day I tried it on for size, Mr. Lynch happened by. As he came in, we were centering Mama's locket. We knew the locket had to be part of her daughter's first bridesmaid outfit.

He spun me around in a circle, exclaiming, "I declare, Miss Ociee, but you do look beautiful. Wonderful job, Mamie."

I curtsied. "Thank you, sir." Aunt Mamie beamed.

"I believe this outshines Ociee's parade outfit."

"Why you know me, George, I always endeavor to better myself."

There I was looking in the mirror. Looking out at me was an almost grownup girl covered head to toe in pink satin. The gown was tied with a sash made into a bow, but not in the back like a little girl's dress. The bow was in front like a princess, or maybe like even a Vanderbilt would wear.

"There. I want everyone to see my locket. Thank you, Aunt Mamie."

She replied, "We can do no more, dearest, or you'll surpass Fred's bride!"

"Would that be bad?"

"Yes!"

"Maybe one of these days, I'll be the bride. Do you promise to make that dress for me, too?"

"Yes, darling, of course, I will."

As our train slowed for the terminal in Chattanooga, I peeked into the top of Aunt Mamie's bag. I saw the pink of my dress. It was squished up and would surely need a good ironing.

If I didn't grow too much more, I could wear the dress for my own wedding. I quickly let go of that plan. After all, I was still only eleven years old. At that time, what was most important to me was to find out if I were almost as big as Ben. My own wedding plans would have to wait for another day; and that day was a long, long way down the road.

I made certain I had my ticket for the next train. I hooked Aunt Mamie's basket over my arm, tied tight my hat, and picked up the traveling bag. As I stepped out of the passenger car, I paused on the step-down. Smiling at the conductor, I said, "Thank you very much, sir."

I should try to behave every bit as politely as Rebecca. After all, we were going to be sisters.

8

It seemed to me that the depot in Chattanooga had grown even bigger and noisier than when I came through the first time. My knees began to shake. I surely didn't want to appear frightened, so I took in a deep breath and swallowed hard. Just then, I spotted a girl who was about my age. She was walking next to her mother. I remembered seeing them when they got on the train. Thinking they were headed for the terminal, I followed in behind them. I wondered if that girl knew how blessed she was to have her mother with her.

As far as my eyes could see, folks were milling about like ants on a mound. Some hollered and hugged "hello," while others cried and waved "good-bye." Still others walked along trying not to get lost. I was one of those. When I could no longer keep up with the girl and her mother, I panicked. Suddenly caught up in a gully washer of people, I was being swept down a swollen river to goodness only knew where.

A voice called out my name! Was I only hoping?

Again? Did he say "Ociee"? I couldn't tell certain. Other voices yelled over that man's.

"Ociee!" the voice shouted.

I desperately searched the river of faces.

"Ociee Nash, over here!"

Could there be another Ociee Nash? I squinted my eyes and looked toward the voice. The man walked like my Papa. The front of his blond hair curled out from under his cap the very same way Papa's curled out from his hat. But it wasn't my Papa. The man broke through the crowd.

"Ociee, girl, you come here to me!"

"Fred? Fred!" I screamed as I dropped all my belongings and raced into the strong arms of my big brother. Fred picked me up and swung me around like a sack of feed. All the while he was squeezing me tight, Fred repeated my name over and over again.

"Ociee, you're here at last!"

I near about got dizzy from the swinging and from the joy of his feel, his smell, his holding me close.

I grinned as he put me down. "Land sakes, Fred Nash, you sure know how to surprise a person."

"That was the idea. And there's more."

My mouth dropped open. "More? What is it, Fred? Is Rebecca with you?" The air left me at the thought of sharing him.

"No, little sister, I want us to be by ourselves. I'm spending this time with you," he explained. "The news is that we'll be riding together all the way to Abbeville."

"Oh, Fred, do you mean it, do you really mean it?" I shrieked so loud that folks passing looked funny at me, maybe at the both of us. Fred noticed, too, because he blushed a bit.

"'Course, I do. Now, come on, let's find us something to eat and do some talking." Fred picked up the things I'd flung. Taking my bag, he handed me the basket and put his arm around my shoulder. I felt safe.

"Well, Ociee, that is, if you still like to talk?"

"Reckon I do! Sometimes I talk so much to Aunt Mamie, she complains that her ears turn red."

"Good then, nothing much has changed. Except I believe that you've grown about a foot, and you've gotten a might pretty."

"Fred, do you really think so? Am I tall as Ben? And pretty, too?"

"You wouldn't want to be as tall as that beanpole Ben!"

"You really think I'm pretty?"

"Sure do."

I didn't know what pleased me more, being pretty or growing a foot.

I had no idea what time it was. I just knew we were sitting in a nice restaurant, and for a whole night's train ride my big brother was mine. I grinned. I never could recall what we ate for supper; I just remembered floating up out of my seat as I realized I was sitting across from my Fred. We two caught up with more than a year and a half of lost time.

My family could write me letters until their fingers curled to knots, but watching them as they spoke was the surest way for me to understand what they were saying. I needed to see how a person's face changed. Papa taught me that. He always said, "The truth in a person comes through his eyes."

I'd made some notes about truth in my journal. One of the best examples concerned a boy and a girl from my school. I was careful not to mention their names, because these weren't very nice stories.

Every time _____ fibs to our teacher, his jaw begins to twitch. The bigger the tale, the more he twitches. Miss Small noticed, too, because she is wise.

There is also a girl who rocks back and forth on her heels when she fibs about her missing homework. Today, ___ told me she didn't even do it, and then she told Miss Small it got lost on the way to school. All the time, she was just a rocking away. Miss Small caught her and sent her directly to the corner!!

Miss Small! Gracious goodness, I thought about my school lessons. I promised her that if she would give permission for me to be gone an entire month, I'd keep up with my assignments. I hadn't done one minute's worth of English or spelling since I left Asheville. If it were the truth I was thinking about, I'd best be "truthful" and keep my own good word to my Miss Small.

I promised myself I'd get to those lessons as soon as I got settled at home.

I looked over at Fred eating his supper. Of course, my brother wouldn't be telling fibs. That was for sure. But still, I wanted to watch my brother talk, if only for the joy of seeing him.

"Oh, Fred, you can't mean it!" I squealed. Once again the other diners turned and glared at me.

Fred smiled at them and said, "She's fine, just an excitable girl."

That made me mad as fire. I stood up and explained myself. "Excitable? Horse feathers! You ought to listen to all the interesting stories he's telling me. My brother is an honest-to-gosh train engineer-in-training. Why, he just said...," but before I got to finish my sentence, Fred patted my hand.

"Quiet down, Ociee, folks are trying to enjoy their own conversations. Besides, we should be finishing up. It wouldn't do for us to miss our train, would it?"

I knocked over my water as I grabbed for Aunt Mamie's basket. I wasn't thirsty anyhow. As we passed by the table next to ours, I stopped and spoke to the four folks eating dessert. "My brother is going to build his very own railroad company. Maybe, just maybe, he'll allow you to take a ride." I stuck up my nose and walked off.

Fred made an embarrassed face. Securing our tickets in his coat pocket, he caught up with me, took my hand, and we hurried on our way. I didn't bother to look out for the first sign as Fred and I brushed past all those slow pokes that didn't have the slightest ideas where they were going. I simply loved it. I was Ociee Nash, and my brother was taking me home.

"Fred Nash, is that you?"

We stopped. Fred greeted the man with a grownup sounding "Hello, there!" After I nudged him just a bit, my brother introduced me.

"Edward, this is my sister, Miss Ociee Nash."

The fellow took my hand and shook it, so I shook his back. I shook it so hard my hat fell forward. The dern thing dropped down over my face and caught on the end of my nose. That Edward was real nice about it, however; he acted as if he hadn't noticed my awkward moment.

"Ociee has already come all the way from Asheville today," explained Fred. "Now the two of us are on our way home to Mississippi. We're leaving tonight on an 8 o'clock run."

"Mighty fine. Tell me, Fred, did I hear you're getting married?"

"Indeed you did! In two weeks. I am one lucky man, because Rebecca Hutchinson will become Mrs. Fred Nash."

My brother bragged some about his Rebecca. I was busy fixing my hat back in place. I tied it tight under my chin and pretended to be interested in their conversation. Aunt Mamie taught me to pay attention to what others were saying. She emphasized, "It is good manners to listen."

The train's whistle tooted. "Ociee, that's for us!"

"Nice to meet you," I said. I was being polite again. I hadn't had near enough time to know if Edward was nice or not.

As we were leaving the man, he chuckled, "Nash, don't you be getting nervous come that wedding day!"

"I'm as calm as, as, as, as…," My brother started acting crazy, like he was all tensed up. I didn't understand that one bit. He'd seemed perfectly all right to me until his friend made that remark.

For once I was glad for a train's whistle calling to me. I was ready to go. Usually the whistle was a sad sound, but this time, the lonesome sound was calling us home.

As we quickly walked along, I asked Fred what was making him nervous. "Don't you like Rebecca anymore?"

"How'd you come up with that?"

"Reckon because you got all shaky with Edward."

Fred didn't respond to my concern; he only laughed.

At that moment, I decided my brother was a sure enough adult. Elizabeth and I were right when we figured out that people who are a good bit older than us didn't always make sense. Fred Nash was grown all right.

I was looking forward to the wedding, and especially to the party afterwards. I'd been to several weddings in Asheville. Always, Aunt Mamie, Mr. Lynch, and I got dressed in our Sunday best. Once the ceremonies were over, we'd go to the party, eat cake, and drink cup after cup of fruit punch.

At one wedding the guests were invited to dance. We danced; actually we only *tried* to dance. Mr. Lynch and Aunt Mamie's attempt was one of the funniest things I ever saw. He kept stomping on her green satin toes. All the while, she hopped about trying to avoid his feet without offending his efforts. When my aunt decided to sit down, Mr. Lynch took my hand.

"No, sir, I don't know how!" I protested. "Aunt Mamie has only just begun to teach me."

"I'll show you, Ociee, it's easy." Reluctantly I followed him onto the floor. The music began. "One, two, three, one two, three." I tried hard to do what he told me, but I was clumsy as an old cow.

"Moo, Mr. Lynch!"

"Did you say 'move'?" he asked.

"No, sir, I said MOO!"

"Fred, will we have to dance at your wedding?"

"No, the reception will be in the parlor of the Hutchinsons' church. Thank the Lord, too, because I have two left feet."

"You have two left feet!" I giggled, "And your sister has hoofs!"

We hurried along laughing. The months of separation melted; and before I knew it, we were climbing aboard our train.

"Come on, girl, let's go home!"

As we waited to depart, I reached into my bag and pulled out Mama's portrait. Taking the picture, my bother gasped. "Ociee! This is the picture the gypsy man gave to you! Why, it looks exactly like Mama."

"See, Fred, see how she smiles? The gypsy painted it so I could remember Mama's face the way it was, not like the frowning one in the parlor."

"Lordy, girl, I'll never forget the day that man came to the farm. Papa nearly had a fit about him scaring you and Ben. Then if that gypsy didn't turn around and paint this beautiful picture just for you. Beats anything I ever saw."

"Fred, Papa taught us not to size up folks by their looks."

Fred quietly caressed the picture with his fingers.

As we pulled out of the depot and headed towards Lookout Mountain, I told Fred about the famous battle they'd fought there during the War. "It must have been a horrible fight, Fred; so many men were killed, including Mr. Charles's own brother. *Mr. Charles!*" I hollered. "I clean forgot to look for Mr. Charles in Chattanooga!"

"Mr. Charles? Oh yes, that kind conductor. You wrote home about him. He looked after you on your trip from Abbeville."

I told Fred every thing I could recall about the nice man. My brother asked questions about Mr. Charles, and I was all too happy to answer. "I believe Mr. Charles paid more attention to me than he did to any of the other passengers!"

Fred grinned.

"Mr. Charles said I was the most interesting child. You understand, Fred, I was much younger back then."

"I can only imagine what the run must have been like for Mr. Charles!" chuckled Fred.

We settled ourselves for the long ride. I had looked forward to watching out the window and seeing again the same sights I had seen before. But it was dark so I couldn't see. The truth was, I was so happy to be with Fred, there wasn't much that could have disappointed me that night.

"By the way," commented my brother. "Aunt Mamie sent Rebecca and me the nicest present. It's a sterling silver serving spoon with the letter 'N' engraved on the handle."

"I know. We picked it out together. 'N' is for Nash, because you have to share the spoon with Rebecca and she has to take *our* name. Aunt Mamie told me so. Reckon Rebecca likes that all right? I wouldn't want to give up being Ociee Nash."

"Doesn't seem to bother her."

Fred also mentioned the message that accompanied the gift. "I can see why you've been so happy with Aunt Mamie. She's very dear. Along with the spoon, she included a thoughtful letter of well wishes. In it, she also mentioned her Ociee."

"Me?"

"Yes, indeed, she told me exactly when you would be traveling. In fact, that was what started me to thinking that I might surprise you."

"I'm so glad you did, Fred."

"I wish Aunt Mamie could have come, too. And so does Rebecca. Of course, she went on and on about how sorry she was about not being able to be with us for the wedding. In fact, I just posted a letter back to thank her. I also suggested that I, er, that is, *we*, Rebecca and I, will plan on going to Asheville for a visit."

"Fred! But you must wait for me to get back! I have to be there to greet you. We'll pick you up in Mr. Lynch's buggy and have a grand party so you can meet everyone. Elizabeth will be so excited!" I jumped onto my knees in the seat. I squeezed his neck. "When?"

"Hold your horses, girl. You're not even to Mississippi as yet!"

"Guess I got a tad ahead of things." I settled back into my seat.

"Just a tad. But don't fret, because you will be the first to know when we can come."

That settled, I got to thinking that I should explain about Aunt Mamie and how busy she always was. "I'm glad you wrote to her. Once she reads that you aren't too disappointed, Aunt Mamie can let loose her worry over letting you and Rebecca down."

"I wish she hadn't worried."

The time seemed right to again ask my brother about his fretfulness.

Fred turned pinkish as he tried to assure me. "Ociee, not one thing is troubling me. Any jitters only means I want everything to turn out well." My brother became a totally different person as he went on and on about the romantic stuff. When he got to describing the cottage they'd have in Memphis, I couldn't help it—I yawned.

Fred poked me. "Ociee, bored, are you? Better watch out, because one of these days, both you and Ben will have your own sweethearts, too. You won't be yawning then."

"I reckon." I yawned again.

He laughed.

"I want to hear all about you, Ociee."

"Not now, Fred, first tell me more of your train stories, not so much about how hard you had to work putting down those cross ties. That's too akin to planting crops, and I know all about that!"

"Planting crops is the same as laying ties? That's a funny one, Ociee!"

"Being the fireman and fueling the engine near about by yourself. That's what I want to hear. Oh please!"

Fred didn't mind talking. He cared about his railroading, and he liked to brag about his steady climb toward to becoming an honest-to-gosh engineer. It seemed to me that he cared about trains as much as he cared about Rebecca. Sitting there as Fred recounted railroad stories made me believe I was riding along with him on his runs back and forth from Memphis to New Orleans. He talked and I listened way into the night.

Close to ten o'clock, he asked, "Do you want to hear the creepiest thing that ever happened?"

"Do I like apple pie! 'Course I do!"

The conductor came by and interrupted us. "Nice having another railroad man riding with us, Nash."

Fred passed him a note of some kind. I couldn't have been less interested. I only wished the friendly man would leave us by ourselves so my brother could tell his story.

"Is it about a ghost, Fred?" I turned my face nose to nose with his and pulled my knees up under my chin.

"Let's see, well, maybe she was on her way to becoming one."

Mouth wide opened, I asked, "She?"

"Let's see, I was coming back from New Orleans," he began. "Are you sure you want to hear this?"

"Fred!"

"Guess you do." He opened wide his eyes and made a growling face. "Well, this happened last spring. It had been raining for days on end, and there'd been a good bit of flooding all through the farmlands down south of Memphis. That evening our train's engineer had us taking things at an unusually slow pace. It was early evening and the sun was about to go down. I'd been shoveling coal into the fire and stopped briefly to wipe my face. I also took a big gulp of water. It was at that very moment something ahead caught my eye."

I listened. My imagination was moving a whole lot faster than the old train. "Fred! It was an alligator! I just know it. Did you see an alligator, Fred? How big was he? Was his mouth wide open?"

"No! We were too far north for any old alligator to travel." Fred shushed me. "Even though what I saw was a good distance away, it appeared to be a box of some kind. I pointed it out to our engineer, so he slowed our train all the more. As we got closer, he and I both could make out that there were a good number of boxes. Ociee, you may not believe this, but what we were looking at was a blooming bunch of coffins!"

"Dead folks!" I yelled.

Passengers sitting anywhere in ear range of us leaned forward in their seats, and others turned around. Everyone was gawking at my brother and me. Anyone who wasn't listening before surely was then.

Fred raised his hand as if he were taking an oath. "There was no mistaking it, those were coffins. Some were fairly old, too, judging from the various stages of decay."

Decay. I wouldn't let myself think about that.

"I'd not seen anything like this before and hope to never again," declared Fred. He went on to mention that his train's engineer had the same awful experience with his own kinfolks. He explained to Fred that his family had to go back and rebury all the bodies.

"So seeing those coffins upset the poor engineer all the more," added Fred.

My eyes filled with tears. To me, it was horrible enough to bury folks the first time. I didn't want to hear about that, and Fred understood why. It was because of Mama. He recognized my troubled look.

"Now, Ociee, I didn't mean to get you worked up. There's no need for you to worry. Mama is buried way up on that hill in Abbeville. There's no river near enough to flood. Besides, you know full well, she is safe in Heaven."

"I know," I whispered. I noticed other passengers still listening, and suspected they were fearful their own kin could be floating around in the Delta, too. I was mighty glad for Mama's high hill, and I was even gladder for Heaven.

"Now about the part of the story Ben liked the most. You want me to go on?"

"Ben's favorite part?" Hearing Ben's name perked me up. "Yes, please!"

He began, "Ociee, did you know that sometimes fancy coffins have windows?"

"Windows? So the dead person can look out?"

He laughed. "No, you goose, a dead person can't see!" Fred laughed again. "The window is so the family can have one last look at the person."

"Oh."

The people around us were chuckling, too. Fred put his hand under my chin. "Lord, girl, I'd forgotten how funny you are! I have missed my Ociee something awful."

"I missed you, too, Fred." I hugged him. But then I got to thinking about Fred's story and jerked away. "Go on, Fred, and tell me the rest!"

"All right then."

The train's wheels click-clacked under us.

"As our train passed those coffins, we were going so slow we were about stopped still. I counted nine, maybe ten coffins all together," he paused. "A couple of them were almost covered over by the water. So I figured there could have been even more out there."

"The coffin closest to the train was one of those fancy kinds I told you about, the kind with the window," he repeated. "Ociee, it was getting dark, mind you, so it was getting harder for me to see. But when I looked down at it, I saw the strangest sight. I saw the face of a dead lady!"

"Looking at you! With her eyes open?" I screamed. "How scary! Did you holler?"

By then, I was up on my feet with my nose all but touching his. Fred tried to quiet me by answering fast my questions. "Shh! Of course not, she wasn't scary, and her eyes were closed. As I recall, she appeared older than me, but younger than our Mama, maybe somewhere in her thirties. The lady was real peaceful like, as if she was sleeping."

"Gracious, I can't wait to write Elizabeth! Now, Fred, tell me, what exactly did Ben say about this?"

"Oh, he was real excited, about like you, and had a bunch of questions, too." Fred smiled. "A couple of weeks afterwards, Ben rode the train back home from Memphis. He was so determined to find his *own* dead person, he nearly fell out the window searching every cotton field he passed!"

I pressed my nose to the window. "Fred, I can't see a blooming thing; it's way too dark out."

"Thank the good Lord for that. I wouldn't want to worry about losing you this close to home!"

9

Fred showed me his pocket watch. "Getting near to midnight, Ociee," he said with a yawn.

My eyes fluttered shut, but I opened them as fast as I could. Fighting sleep, I spit on my fingers and rubbed the wet onto my eyelids. I blinked myself wide-awake and looked out the window. I was on the watch for coffins.

Every so often, I'd spot a cabin or a house with a candle burning in the window. For the most part, though, it appeared all of Tennessee had gone to sleep. I squiggled down in my seat and snuggled my head next to Fred's big shoulder. How like Papa he suddenly felt to me.

"Ready to get some rest, Ociee?"

"No, not at all." Even so, I resolved myself to get quieter so my brother could sleep.

A voice sounded over the rhythmic chugging of the train's wheels. "My little friend Ociee, it *is* you!"

I turned in my seat.

"Well, I'll be!" the man's voice said. "You did come along for another ride on my train. You kept your promise."

"Mr. Charles, are you sure you are you?"

"There's not another conductor in this world I could be but me," he beamed, patting his ample belly. "Although, you might notice there is a good bit more of your old Mr. Charles these days!"

I giggled. He was right; he was a whole heap fatter.

Mr. Charles shook his head. "Indeed, Ociee Nash, it is such a marvelous surprise to see you. Did you know that the thanks are due to your brother? Fred Nash, this must be."

Fred and I both answered, "Yes, it's Fred."

"He's Fred, I'm Ociee!" I said it in real giddy way. I was feeling silly all over because of the wonderful surprises happening to me.

"You are still a delight, my dear." Mr. Charles smiled sweetly and continued, "I must apologize for taking so long to get to you. By the time your brother's message got to my end of the train, I was too busy to leave. Got here fast as I could."

Mr. Charles turned to Fred and thanked him.

"Mighty nice to meet you, too, sir. Our family is most grateful for the attention you paid to our girl."

"The pleasure was all mine, young man. Say, I understand you've become a railroad man yourself?"

"Yes, Mr. Charles, indeed I have! I'm out of Memphis."

They talked as I watched. My dreams were all coming true at once. Even though I had only known Mr. Charles for a few hours during that first train ride, he had been my friend when I was the most fearful and lonely as I'd been in my whole life. He'd talked with me every chance he could. I probably took too much of his time; I understood that after our Fred joined the railroad. In his letters telling us about his work, I realized what Mr. Charles had done for me.

Fred got up to give my friend his seat. "Believe me, I need to stretch these long legs. Besides, that will give the two of you a chance to visit. I might just wander the length of your train." He added, "Please don't concern yourself for a minute, Mr. Charles. I'll be certain to let you know if there's any problem in your area."

"Very nice of you, young man," he remarked, "but I doubt there will be much to give us worry. If my recollection is clear, any excitement on this train will take place wherever your little sister happens to be!"

I giggled thinking of the stir I caused in the depot in Holly Springs. Fred walked through the door to the platform outside and disappeared into the next car.

"Mr. Charles, I'd guess you're remembering when my gypsy friend rode up on his big black horse to say good-bye?"

"Missy, back when you got on my train in Abbeville, I promised your Papa I'd watch out for you. First stop out, here comes this big fierce-looking gypsy fellow shouting out your name! Nearly stopped my heart, he did."

"But he was all kindness on his inside."

"So you said. And that was just the beginning to a most unusual run for me. One of the most amusing in my years as a conductor, I'd venture!" He paused. "Asheville, wasn't Asheville where you were heading after my turnaround in Chattanooga? I thought I remembered that from the tag your people had pinned to your dress."

I smiled at recalling how determined I had been to make certain I kept "who I was and where I was going" securely attached to me. I believed losing that tag meant losing Ociee.

"Yes, it was Asheville, Mr. Charles. And it has turned out to be a good place for me. That is, once I got accustomed to being so far away from home. I have a very best friend there named Elizabeth Murphy. My Aunt Mamie, well," I hesitated. "I have too much to tell you, Mr. Charles! For example, on this day, I'm on my way home for Fred's wedding. The wedding isn't today, of course. Our Fred is getting married on March the third."

Mr. Charles nodded.

"I'll be going back to North Carolina in a month." I could barely take in air for talking so fast. "Will you ride with me again? Please, Mr. Charles, say you will? 'Course, now, it won't be quite the same as last time, because I'm mighty grown up now. See, no tags for me! I'm near about twelve, truly, Mr. Charles, in nine more months, I will be."

"I'm sorry to say, Ociee, but I'm getting ready to retire. I have only two more weeks on this job. It was a blessing I got to see you at this time."

I wondered why happy so often got stomped on by sad. I could have cried when he told me.

Mr. Charles went on to say he was looking forward to retiring and that he was anxious to begin working his small farm. I warned him about Papa and how, even working as hard as he could, he had lost our farm. I also mentioned how much happier Papa was being a smart bookkeeper at Fitch's Mercantile. Mr. Charles explained that his farm wasn't going to be a large one like ours.

"I will miss this train," he admitted. "Ociee, it's been my whole life for more than thirty years."

"Gracious sakes, thirty years! You are old, aren't you?" I forgot every manner I'd ever been taught.

He laughed. I was glad.

"I'll miss the honesty of charming passengers like you." He patted my cheek. "Don't you ever think of losing that quality of yours, you hear? By the way, that reminds me, young lady, I well remember your many questions. Tell me, are you still so curious?"

"My Aunt Mamie, you remember, I was going to stay with Papa's sister, Mamie Nash?"

"Of course."

"My aunt would say, '*For certain*, Ociee is as curious as ever.' She says the wheels in my brain just never cease their turning. Sometimes, she will stop what she's doing and caution me, 'Ociee, don't allow your mouth to talk faster than your brain's wheels can turn!'"

"My dear, but you are a sight! Now won't you please tell me all about your adventures in North Carolina? I cannot imagine that the state is quite the same since your arrival."

Mr. Charles asked, so I was pleased as punch to tell him. Going from front to back, I began by giving him every detail about our parade, including all about Mr. Lynch and Old Horse.

"How I'd enjoy seeing that horse in his hat!" he responded.

Then I shared Papa's visit last year. I again voiced some concern about Mr. Charles's farm.

"My dear child, you are absolutely not to worry yourself about me. I promise I could always return to this job."

I felt better right away wishing he'd be back with the railroad for my trip home.

I always liked to talk about Elizabeth. When I got to the part about her fire and how terrifying it was, Mr. Charles was just trembling. He shook his head back and forth, and acted as scared as if he were there that dreadful night. I didn't ask him; but in my heart, I knew he'd been through something just as awful. The look in his eyes said I was right.

Then, after I told him what the community had done for the Murphys, Mr. Charles grinned ear-to-ear. "Sounds like people in Asheville are most generous."

"Yes, sir, we are!"

The last thing I brought up was the Vanderbilts. Being a trainman himself, he knew exactly who they were. Mr. Charles told me the Vanderbilts' home came from railroad money.

"That's good news for Fred!"

Thinking back, I might have exaggerated some, because in my telling of things, Mr. Charles might have gotten the idea we were all real good friends; the Vanderbilts, Elizabeth, Aunt Mamie, Mr. Lynch, and me.

By the time Fred returned, I was ready to suggest one last thing to Mr. Charles. I went on and said it, even though Fred might have thought me bossy. "Should you change your mind about your farming, and you decide against being a conductor again, why don't you come to Asheville? I am certain Mr. Lynch could find you a carriage along with a real good horse."

Without giving him a second to respond, I explained, "Mr. Charles, driving a buggy would be worlds more interesting for you than doing all those farm chores. All's you'd have to do would be to ride around picking up folks and taking them where they ask to go. 'Course, you'd need to feed and groom your horse. I'd be pleased as peaches to teach you everything about it."

Mr. Charles and Fred were laughing their heads off. I didn't see the first funny thing about my plan.

Fred quit chuckling long enough to comment, "I 'spect I should have left you to your own sleeping passengers, Mr. Charles. It appears that my sister is wanting to turn your life inside out."

"What, and miss such a delightful visit? I think not. I'm enjoying every minute with this child."

It disappointed me that my friend called me a *child*. I wrinkled up my brow.

He may have noticed because of what he said next. "Ociee is a clever *young lady*. In fact, if my dear wife weren't so determined to keep these feet of mine planted deep in the soil of the Delta, I'd possibly take your sister's advice."

"See, Fred, Mr. Charles did pay attention to my suggestion!" I had to gloat.

"It seems so," he admitted.

Acting so cocky like I did must have meant there was still a good amount of "child" left in me after all. I'd have to work on my gloating.

"Ociee, as much as I don't want to leave your wonderful company, it's best I be getting back to work. I haven't retired as yet, you see." Mr. Charles tipped his hat. "I cannot begin to tell you how much I have enjoyed our visit. I do promise to keep your idea in my mind."

"Mr. Charles, thank you for visiting with me." I added, "Thank you, too, for my first trip. You may not have noticed, but I was a tiny bit nervous. Fact is, you kept me from flying apart like a dandelion in a windstorm."

Mr. Charles smiled sweetly as Fred looked knowingly at me and winked.

"Whatever do you mean, Ociee? I didn't notice any nervousness. In my opinion, you were most confident. You also provided me with absolutely charming company, just as you have this night."

He turned to my brother. "Mr. Nash, thank you again for letting me know we had a special passenger on board." He shook Fred's hand, saying, "Best luck to you with the railroad, son." With that Mr. Charles gave Fred his seat, said good-bye, and walked away.

As soon as he was out of sight, I said, "I know I'm right, Fred, Mr. Charles would make a fine carriage driver."

"What, and give Mr. Lynch competition? After all, George Lynch is practically a member of our family."

"Oh dear, I hadn't thought about that."

"Are you sleepy *yet*, little sister?"

"Not in the least."

"Me neither."

In minutes, we both were sound asleep like everyone else in western Tennessee.

10

A jolt, a lunge, then came the shattering CRASH!

My head banged on something in front of me. Everything around us was dark as tar. Fred? I couldn't find my brother! I tried to escape, but I couldn't budge from my seat. I was trapped!

"*Fred!*" I needed to holler, but my voice wouldn't let me. Once again, I opened wide my mouth to call out for help.

No matter how hard I tried, I could make no sound. What happened? I attempted to see through the thick darkness. I reached out and hit glass. What? The window. Still, I couldn't see a thing. The train? Was I still on the train? Where, oh where, was my brother?

"Dear Lord," I realized, "I am in a coffin."

As hard as I pushed the glass to free myself, I could not budge the heavy door. Exactly like that lady Fred saw in the water, the dead lady; I was trapped. Yet I wasn't asleep like her. I wasn't peaceful like Fred told me the lady was. I was wide awake and terrified to my bones. The dark had swallowed me. They had buried their Ociee, and I knew I was still alive! The river was coming up over my ears. I could feel it washing against the back of my head.

I tried one more time to scream. "Help!" I shouted at the top of my lungs and finally broke through the awful silence.

I flung out my arms. Mercifully Fred grabbed for me.

"Fred, get me out of here! The river is coming!"

"Ociee? Wake up, girl!"

I trembled with fear as my brother held me tight.

"Ociee, you've had a bad dream."

"Dream?"

"It's all right, Ociee. You are safe," he repeated. "Just a dream, was all, just a bad dream."

"But I couldn't find you! I couldn't even holler."

"You hollered, all right! Look, you woke up everyone in our car."

"The car?"

Sure enough, the other passengers were eyeing me with the oddest expressions. Some seemed concerned; while the others were plain irritated. Their frowns said so. I was glad Fred was sitting there with me.

"Everything is fine," Fred told the folks. "My sister's just had a nightmare."

"A nightmare?" I was still groggy.

"Glory be, little sister, when you came to, you were beating on the window. I thought you'd spotted a coffin out in the middle of a cornfield!"

I tried to speak, but I was still shaking so much that forming words was near about impossible. Eventually, I calmed down enough to talk. "Fred I was dreaming I was *in* a coffin! It was one of those you told me about, the kind with a window. All I wanted was out!"

"Good thing you didn't break the glass."

"It was gosh awful terrible! Fred, I don't remember ever dreaming such a scary dream."

"This brother will *not* be telling you any more stories. And that, Ociee Nash, is a promise."

"But I like your stories."

"Let's say then, as a kindness for others, we'll avoid them this trip?"

"All right. I guess."

"By the way, you might like to know we'll be pulling into Holly Springs in just over an hour. That means Papa and Ben are likely readying themselves to come to meet us."

My dreadful dream popped like a soap bubble in the Monday wash.

Finally, I could watch as the sun came up on my Mississippi! As though the Lord had lit a giant candle, I could see the countryside bathed in orange and pink. Every barn, every house, every outbuilding we passed, even ones just built, felt familiar to me. I reckon that was because I wanted so for home to feel like home.

As the train churned fast through the flat farmlands, I wanted to lean out and wave hello to every cow, every bird, and every chicken, but the chilly morning forced me to shut my window. After all, I didn't need to be freezing my nose off and ruin my homecoming.

Cows mooed, "You're home, Ociee." The roosters cock-a-doodle-dooed their welcomes to me. Even though it was past sunrise, and their day's wakeup call was accomplished, those roosters knew this hometown girl was back.

The morning frost glistened like gold in the gray mist. I realized that the farmers were seeing to their chores; still, I told myself, they had to be taking note of the train with Ociee Nash on board.

Fred and I shared a breakfast of bread with the last of Aunt Mamie's marmalade smeared thin on top, along with bananas, juice, and a sweet cake my brother brought in his lunch tin.

Fred said, "I believe I prefer being a guest of the railroad instead of stoking coal into the engine."

I argued with him about that. "That can't be true. It has to be more fun to be running the train. I wish we were up in front with the engineer, Fred. I could help you be his fireman!"

"Ociee, such a thing would be against every safety railroad rule there is. I can see us now, if you were helping me shovel that coal. You'd be having us go so fast, we would run straight through to Texas. Why, girl, you'd likely make us my wedding!"

Fred was right; I was about to bust to get home.

"Oh, Fred, how much longer 'til we're there?"

"Girl, it hasn't been two minutes since you asked the last time."

"It's been at least five."

"Afraid not, little sister."

"I almost wish you hadn't told me we were getting close. The time's passing like old honey on a cold biscuit." I wiggled in my seat. I was getting mighty worn out from sitting.

Fred offered to tell another story.

"A scary one?"

"No, ma'am!"

"But, Fred, I wouldn't get afraid this hour of the morning. See, because the sun is out," I begged him.

My brother wouldn't give in, saying he really wanted to reminisce about the days when we were little. Actually, I was happy about that. Our old times were too far away for me to recall, and a girl like me needed a reminder every now and again.

Fred began to tell me about an event that took place around 1893, way back before our Mama got sick. He was twelve at the time, not much older than I was then. It was very strange to think of my brother being my age. He'd always seemed real old to me, more like he was an extra Papa.

"Ociee, you were a little thing," he began, "nearly four. You, Ben, me, Mama, and Papa—we all climbed into the wagon and rode the seven miles into Oxford for the county fair."

He painted such a vivid picture of the day. I could almost taste the fall of the year. I saw leaves blowing from the trees and smelled the fresh roasted peanuts as we passed by row after row of baked pies and cakes displayed on cloth-covered tables. As Fred continued, I could all but feel the hay crunching under my feet and listen to the sound of cows mooing and pigs grunting, seemingly unaware of the folks who were milling around among them. Fred told me that nearly every person from a two-county area had traveled to that fair.

"Fred, I'd been real nervous if I'd been a cow waiting on being judged."

"Best you're not," he grinned. "You'd have pitched a fit if you hadn't won the Blue Ribbon."

"If I were a cow, I would have won!"

"Reckon so. But that's the story I want to tell you. You were much too young to remember, Ociee, but I did enter a contest. You see, ribbons were awarded to the livestock, chickens, too; and there were prizes given to the ladies for their baking and for things they made."

I interrupted, "Like quilts? Did Mama's quilt win the prize?"

"I don't remember."

"I just know it did," said I.

"Likely. Mama made beautiful things all right." he sighed.

"Anyhow, they also had races and contests for the young folks and men. I got to watching one contest in particular. One feller after another tried to shinny up a greased pole after an American flag. The pole, slippery from top to bottom, got bigger and bigger towards the top. Men and some boys tried it, but every time a feller would get part way up, he'd start slipping, and zippedy-do, down he'd come!

"I stepped forward. Mind you, at age twelve pushing thirteen, I was real skinny and limber, too. I was built a lot like Ben, and every bit as skinny and every bit as determined. Papa told me later that the higher I got, the larger the crowd grew. I could hear them all cheering for me, too!"

As Fred told me the story, I could tell he was puffing up with pride. "The Nash family was cheering the loudest. 'Go, go, Fred, go!' Of course, Mama was urging me to be careful; and I can still hear Papa as he shouted, 'You can do it, boy. You can do it, Fred Nash!'"

I tried hard to remember.

"Ociee, I can recall your tiny voice squeaking, 'Fed, Fed.' And, Ben, guess he was almost five then, was running around all through the gathering, getting everyone to watch and yell for his big brother."

I smiled real big.

Fred explained that because so many contestants had attempted to reach the top, the grease had been worn away below a certain point. That made the first part of his climb fairly easy, or so he insisted. However, above that spot, the pole was as slick as it had ever been.

He described what he did. "I dug my knees in, hugged that pole tight as I could, and kept my eyes fixed on that American flag. Not once did I let myself look down. I inched up a little at a time, 'til finally close enough, I clung on with two legs and one arm. I swung my right arm up and grabbed that flag. 'Got it!' I yelled. And with that, I slid down the pole.

"At the bottom, the crowd met me with cheers and shouts of 'Hooray for Fred!' The men carried me on their shoulders all the way to the lemonade stand. I was so proud and happy, my face turned apple red. I wasn't accustomed to having so much attention. Papa was about to bust wide open. Mama cried, more pleased I wasn't hurt. You were clapping, too, and Ben went wild. You'd thought he'd done it."

"I can see him now," I said.

"Of course, I was given all the pink lemonade and ice cream I wanted. On top of that, I'd won the prize. I got to keep the American flag with its stripes and all forty-two stars. Papa has that flag saved for me in a trunk at home."

"I'm proud of you all over again, 'Fed.'"

Fred said he must ask Rebecca if he'd told her about that day. I was sure he had. After all, my brother was smart enough to impress his girl with such an exceptional feat as winning the best prize at the county fair.

Later as we pulled into Holly Springs, I was half expecting to see the gypsy man. But he wasn't there. The beating of my heart quickened as I realized that in less than an hour we'd be making our very last stop. Home! I asked Fred if I had time to get off the train and freshen up. He told me I did.

As I walked around, I felt funny. The bottoms of my feet were tingling and the rest of me was heavy. For certain I'd been on that train too long. I didn't much feel like me. I felt more like a bird who'd been flying around and around in her cage. It was well past time for an Ociee bird to perch somewhere.

I washed up and tried to fix my hair. I finally managed to hide most of it under my hat. I got on and sat back down next to Fred. "I'm ready. Tell the engineer that we can go now."

11

"Fred, I changed my mind."

"About what?"

"I don't want to go home, I feel like I've swallowed a field full of butterflies. What if no one remembers me? I think I'm going to upchuck. Elizabeth upchucked all the way to Georgia."

Fred burst out laughing.

"What's so funny?"

"One minute you're cocky as a rooster; the next, you're skittish as a barn cat."

"Reckon the really and true Ociee is somewhere in the middle."

"Whichever Ociee will feel fine once we get there," my brother encouraged.

As we rode the short distance we had left to travel, I got worse. I made pleading faces at Fred to make me better; but he just shook his head, grinned, and suggested I calm down. When the whistle sounded, I almost fell off my seat. Fred looked at me and said, "Meow."

I opened the window and could just about make out the depot in Abbeville. "We're here!" I shouted, attempting to climb over Fred.

"Best wait 'til we stop, you think?"

"Guess so."

I sat.

"Ociee, I want to say something important to you. Now, and this is hard for me, so please listen," said Fred. "You are my only sister, my dear little sister, and I want you to remember that I will always care about you. Don't mean to get all mush-mouthed here, but I love you very much."

I didn't want to cry. It was too cheerful a moment, so I replied, "I love you, too. Thank you for meeting me." Then I swallowed kind of hard and added, "I'm sorry for all the times I made fun of Rebecca."

"No matter, but you better quit because she'll soon have a husband who will come after you!"

"Husband? Gracious, Fred, you are old!"

Five minutes later the train pulled into the depot. My feet refused to move. My butterflies had wings big enough to fly ducks.

Fred pulled me up by my elbow. "Ociee, I believe there might be a couple of folks wanting to greet you."

I stood speechless so he picked up my traveling bag and my basket and took my hand.

We stepped off the train. Papa stood not ten feet away from us with his arms held open. With tears streaming down my face, I ran to him and buried myself in his chest. As I turned my face, I saw Mr. Charles watching from a distance. I loosed my hand and waved. He waved back.

Still with his left arm around me, Papa reached for Fred. "Good trip, son?"

"Yes, sir, and not boring in the least!"

"I can imagine."

"Hey, Ociee."

I turned my head. Ben walked out from behind a wagon piled high with trunks and bags. Papa and Fred stepped aside as Ben and I slowly edged toward one another. It's strange when the person I had wanted most to see in the world was right there, yet neither one of us knew quite how to be. I had jumped all over Fred and cried on Papa, but Ben? Both of us were wobbly like newborn colts.

Finally, I reached forward and grabbed him. He grabbed me. We hugged tight, then separated real fast as if we had gotten burned on the woodstove.

"Race you to the wagon!" Ben challenged.

"No fair, I don't know where it is!"

Papa looked at Fred. "Some things don't change."

"Maud!" I patted her and stroked her mane. "How are you doing, old girl? It's Ociee. Do you remember me?"

Maud wasn't as fine a horse as Mr. Lynch's, but then she wasn't meant to pull a fancy carriage either. She was a farmer's plough horse through and through, yellowish white with brown markings, and a very sweet and gentle spirit in spite of the hard work that had been demanded of her.

"I 'spect you are one Nash who doesn't miss our farm, aren't you, Maud?"

She snorted.

I couldn't have been more delighted to see a human friend.

On the way home, I sat with Papa. Ben and Fred rode in the back. I knew Ben was on his best behavior, because he didn't fuss about not riding up front. The day seemed just like old times except for that.

I told myself this was truly happening. When a person looks forward to something as long as I'd looked forward to coming home, that person could be in for a letdown. Thank goodness, that didn't happen to me. Holding tight to Papa, I stood up, steadied myself, and screamed, "I am so happy!"

Ben and Fred shouted all the louder, "So are we!"

"And so am I," said Papa. "But, Ociee dear, please sit down. I don't want you to fall off and get hurt."

Later on, I would write about my trip in my journal. I would include the people I met on the train, Fred, and, of course, Papa and Ben. Papa said something as we were riding home that I was certain to add.

Now, Papa had a way with words. An educated man, he had attended the University of North Carolina. I didn't know much about that until I lived with Aunt Mamie, and she shared her thoughts with me. She believed it was a mistake for her brother to leave Asheville and take his Bertie out west. I wasn't sure she was right about that because I knew our family had been mighty happy in Mississippi. However, I had to admit my aunt was right about one thing. She said Papa was much better at expressing himself than he was at running a farm.

I penned his words in my journal on that February evening in 1900: *Papa said, "If I could hold back time by halting the hands on my pocket watch, I'd certainly do so. I only wish I could ride along just as I am at this very moment, George Nash with his beloved children. How I yearn to keep us as near to one another as we are on this blessed morning."*

I simply swooned.

Ben piped up, "I don't know about riding along forever, Papa. I, for one, would get mighty hungry!"

Even Papa had to laugh.

I eased myself over into the back of the wagon next to Ben. "Are you still thinking about leaving home to join the circus?"

"Don't know, exactly, Ociee. I'm always thinking about something new and exciting. Don't know how I'll ever make up my mind. Miss Brown, my teacher, you remember her, don't you?"

"Yep, sure do."

"Well, she told Papa that I was the restless sort. You know what Papa said?"

"Nope."

"Papa said he figured I acted for all the world like himself! He stood right there and told her, 'My Ben will indeed reach the dream that's best for him, Miss Brown. However, it might take this interesting young man a few tries.'"

Papa heard what Ben said and added, "I wanted his teacher to understand that my Ben is fine just the way he is. As well, so is my Ociee. You're growing into such a gracious young girl back east. And our Fred there, he's getting married in a couple of weeks. What a fortunate man am I to be your papa!

"Fact is, I've been bragging about my children to most anyone who comes into Fitch's Mercantile. Homer Fitch said I should make a big sign telling about the Nash children and display it in the store window."

Ben replied, "I know, Papa, your sign can read, 'For sale, the three perfect Nashes, ages 11, 12, 20. Horse comes with them.'"

Fred added, "Boy, 12, eats more than the horse."

I'd anticipated the familiar long ride out to our farm. I couldn't quite get it into my mind that we weren't going where we were supposed to go. The short ride home made me half happy, half sad. As much as I wanted to get somewhere, it was to our old home I yearned to go.

Papa reined in Maud in front of a house. It didn't look like it belonged to a Nash. An in-town house, painted white with green shutters, it was located only fifteen or twenty feet from the road. The porch was small with just enough room for the four of us to sit, five of us counting Rebecca.

We went inside. Ben carried my bag for me, as I followed him to my new room.

"This is my room," Ben began, "but I'll be sleeping with Fred until the wedding. Papa says it's because you're company."

"Company?"

"Yep, Papa said we're supposed to treat you real special."

I liked the special part, but I didn't like hearing I was a visitor to my very own family.

"See, we moved your old bed in for you."

I sat. Its bumps greeted me like a soft lumpy lap.

"Ben," called Papa from the kitchen, "why don't you show your sister around."

"Yes, sir."

Our furniture was the same; and like my bed, the familiar pieces bid me welcome. Mama's washstand, the rocking chair, and their bed were arranged with the chair in the window as it had been on our farm. Yet when I looked out, in place of yard chickens, the barn, and cornfield, I only saw the house next door.

Papa's desk and chair sat across the parlor from the settee; Mama's portrait hung above. I told Ben to wait, and I went to get the smiling Mama. Ben was still jealous that he wasn't home the day the gypsy returned my lost necklace; naturally then, my brother got really mad when the kind man gave me the painting to take to Asheville. At first, Ben was excited to see Mama's face, but just as quickly, he looked away. I figured it was the envy creeping up again.

The formal poise, the one in keeping with the style of the times, showed Mama with such a stern look. I couldn't bear it. Along with her smile, I missed the twinkle in her eyes. I placed the gypsy's image below the fashionable one.

"Ben, the gypsy didn't actually know Mama, so he painted her with my expression."

My brother groaned.

"Ben, do you think about our Mama sometimes?"

"No, and don't you be talking about her either."

Papa called out, "Ben, come help in the kitchen. Ociee, get yourself washed up for lunch. Everything will be ready soon."

Papa must have been reading my mind, because he seemed to know I was feeling left out. He said, "Ociee girl, you'll have plenty to do soon enough; take time to get yourself accustomed to being home."

I heard plates clattering as he got them down from the cabinet. Papa began to sing, "She'll be comin' round the mountain." The sounds of his off-key singing warmed me. "We'll all go out to meet her when she comes," I echoed. I had to wonder if Susannah's mountain was as tall as any in the Blue Ridge.

All in all, I liked the way the house looked. It was nice and tidy; however, it did need some fixing up, the sort a girl would do. I'd be that girl. I had two weeks before the wedding, and I would need something to busy myself besides keeping up with my lessons. I never had been a person who wasted her time. I could almost see Miss Small's face as I thought about my yet untouched schoolwork. Thank goodness I'd have plenty of time for that while Ben was in school and Papa was at work with Mr. Fitch.

I touched the arm of Mama's chair. I was just like her in wanting to keep busy. How often she had eased herself into her chair after a day of cooking, canning vegetables, sewing new dresses or shirts, fixing my hair, hanging sheets on the clothesline, and sweeping out the house. I remember my Mama saying, "I declare, Ociee, that dust turns right around and races in the door behind my skirt."

I started to sit in Mama's chair, but I couldn't allow myself, not yet.

I turned on my heels and joined the men folks in the kitchen. The table was set for lunch with the red checked cloth and Mama's blue and white plates. The room had the feel of home for me, more so than the rest of the house.

"Can I help?"

Ben said, "You better!"

Papa nodded his head.

I put the butter peas on the table and we all sat down in our regular places. Time melted away as Papa said his blessing. "Lord, I thank you most of all for my children and for our finally being together at this table." I thought he was going to cry. "And, Lord, give my Bertie the love of her George, and of her dear Fred, Ben, and Ociee."

Then I thought I might cry. All of a sudden a yellow cat jumped into the middle of the table. It about scared me to death.

"Go, get on down, Tiger," said Ben pushing him onto the floor.

"Who is this?"

"His name's Tiger. I got him last year," said Ben, "He was supposed to replace you!"

"Did he?"

"Nope, he isn't as much of a pest."

I stuck out my tongue.

Papa said, "Please don't tell Bertie about this turn of events, Lord. She never was one who liked a cat on her table."

It felt so good to be home, Tiger and all. I tried to eat, but mostly I looked from Papa to Ben to Fred and back to Papa again. I was home.

"Anybody here?" Rebecca came in the back door. Fred jumped up from his place, moving twice as fast as Ben's cat.

Ben and I started to mimic the expressions on their faces, but Papa stopped us by shaking his finger and putting it to his lips. "Join us for a bite, Rebecca?" he invited. "There's plenty for you."

"It looks wonderful, Mr. Nash. But I must say no. I want to be able to fit into my wedding dress. That Saturday is just around the corner!"

I looked over at Fred, his eyes rounded into full circles, and again, he blushed. I was beginning to worry that my brother's coloring up would become a permanent condition.

"You look a might flushed, son."

I squooched my shoulders and started to giggle. Ben kicked my foot under the table. I kicked back as we both got tickled.

Rebecca changed the subject. She came over to my chair and hugged me. "And how was your trip, little sister?"

I hugged her back but stayed in my seat. Then I decided to be more receptive, so I stood up and said, "Just fine, 'specially when Fred surprised me."

"He's a sweetheart, my Fred."

My brother reddened up again.

"Rebecca, would you like to see my dress?"

"Oh yes!"

I took her by the hand and walked her into my bedroom.

"Ben's letting me have his room, but I do have *my* own bed. Papa wants me to feel at home."

Rebecca smiled in reply.

Opening the bag, I shook out the dress and told her Aunt Mamie had made it. "Needs some ironing, that's all."

"Never mind that, Ociee. Why, it's simply beautiful!" She offered to press it for me, saying, "What else would a big sister do?"

"I don't know anything about having a sister. I just know about brothers, and they wouldn't think of doing any such a thing."

"We'll both need some practice, won't we?"

I noticed Mama's sapphire on Rebecca's finger. "The ring looks real pretty."

"Dear Ociee! Thank you for saying that." She hugged me again, and that time I hugged her like family might.

After we ate, Fred took Rebecca for a walk. Papa, Ben, and I fiddled around in the kitchen cleaning up, but mostly we were enjoying being together. All too soon, however, Papa had to return to Fitch's, and Ben had lessons to complete. I walked around and sat on every chair in our house. Finally, I sat on Mama's. I wondered if anyone else had.

I unpacked and wandered around outside and even got around to studying my spelling words. We shared our second meal together, and that time Rebecca joined us. My brother escorted her home around 7:30. When he returned, Papa sent Ben and me to get ready for bed. "Fred and I have some talking to do without you two's interruptions!"

I believed that "interruption" referred to Ben and Tiger, not to me. I pulled down the covers. "Hello, lumps." I lowered my voice and said, "Welcome home, Ociee Nash."

Ben hollered out his goodnight to me. I lay there and listened to the sounds of home. A while later, I could hear Ben and Fred wrestling around. Just then Papa came in my room. "Been waiting a mighty long while to wish my daughter her sweetest dreams." He carefully placed a log in the fireplace and stoked it with the poker. "Can't be letting you get cold your first night here."

I reached out for Papa. "I missed you so much!" For some dumb reason, I began to cry. "Why's this happening, Papa?"

"The tears, you mean, Ociee? I believe you're crying because you are so glad to be home."

"That shouldn't make for tears."

"Tears of joy, my girl. Those are the sweetest kind."

"Guess they do taste of sugar, Papa."

He sat on my bed for the longest time. I was all talked out and reckon he was, too. We listened to the fire popping in the fireplace. As he was leaving, Papa put on another big log. He kissed my forehead. "Good night, my Ociee."

"Angels on your pillow, Papa," I replied. "That's what Elizabeth's folks say to her when she goes to sleep. I have wanted to share those angels with you for a long time."

"And may those angels grace your pillow, too." He shut the door and I squeezed tight Mama's locket.

The next thing I remembered was looking up and seeing Ben's Tiger in my face. "Good morning to you, little feller." Thank goodness for that cat; had he not come in to inspect the strange person in Ben's room, I'd likely wasted my whole first day sleeping. I lay there petting the cat, thinking through my list of things to do. Quickly getting dressed, I gobbled down a biscuit Papa left for me and went out for a walk.

Abbeville was much the same as it had been. I saw the general store, the Post Office, our train depot, of course; Fitch's Mercantile, and the candy shop that Ben and I always loved. Abbeville had been the biggest place in the world to me. Now I could walk most of the way through it in twenty minutes' time. Unless I stopped to talk to folks. And that I did!

I visited Mr. Hall at the depot. I'd been so excited to see Papa and Ben the day before, I forgot to speak to him. He was a nice man, had white hair and a beard, sort of like Santa Claus. I thought about Elizabeth and the whitewash! I'd write to her that very day. After we talked a minute or two, Mr. Hall said, "Why, Ociee Nash, I believe that you have grown a foot since you left town."

"No, sir," I snickered, "That's what Fred said, too; but I still have only two feet!"

"That's a good one!" He hooted.

"Wish I could stay longer, Mr. Hall, but I have so much to get done today."

He asked me to come back anytime I liked. I told him I'd try, but for certain Papa and I would be by to pick up my ticket home to Asheville. "*Home* to Asheville," I noticed myself saying.

Next I went to the candy shop. There was Miss Ethel, pretty as ever with her red curls piled loosely on top of her head. The way she arranged her hair always reminded me of the brightly colored sweet treats in the jars on her counter.

"No, I won't take a penny for this candy, Ociee" she insisted. "It's your welcome home gift. Don't you be worrying about sharing with Ben either. Trust me, your brother has wangled more than his share of goodies from me."

"I am very sure of that, Miss Ethel!" I thanked her and walked down the street toward Fitch's.

"Good morning, Papa."

"And good morning to you, my darling girl."

As Papa walked from behind the counter, Mr. and Mrs. Fitch hurried out of the back of the store to greet me. They were the dearest couple, yet so oddly matched in my opinion. Tall and fat was Mrs. Fitch; while her husband was short and as skinny as he could be. I could picture them in my Mother Goose book, "Jack Sprat could eat no fat, his wife could eat no lean."

"I say, young lady, but you are a sight for my eyes," said Mrs. Fitch as she removed an apron from around her ample frame. She pulled me close and engulfed my whole self in a soft hug.

"It feels just right to be home."

Mr. Fitch said, "It's good you finally got here, Ociee. George Nash was about to worry himself to death."

"I'm so sorry, Papa!" I apologized. "I didn't mean to let myself sleep so late today. Gracious goodness, how could I have slept through the commotion of Ben's leaving for school?"

"Oh, no, Ociee, you misunderstood," Mr. Fitch corrected me. "I'm not talking about what time you got here this morning. I'm talking about your arrival yesterday. George Nash fretted every minute you were on that train!"

"Oh, that's Papa. He worries, you know."

"Now I wasn't that bad, Homer." Papa reached in his pocket and counted out some coins. "But, speaking of worry, Ociee, here's some money. You must be sure to send our Mamie a telegram right away. We forgot about that yesterday. She'll be ready to skin us both alive."

"Yes, Papa.

"You see, Homer, we Nashes are a family full of fret," said Papa as he sent me on my way.

"I'll be back."

"Come soon, Ociee dear," said Mrs. Fitch.

The telegraph man was a new face to me. In fact, he was about the only person I'd seen in town who hadn't been there before. Even so, he knew Papa and, apparently, he knew a good bit about me, too.

"Little Ociee, are you? I'm Nester, Nester Jones."

"I'm Ociee, that's right. But I'm not so little, as you can see." I wrinkled my brow at him.

He thought that was funny. I should have been angry, but I wasn't because Mr. Jones didn't charge me for sending my message. First, the free candy; then, the free telegram. What a day that was!

I wrote down Aunt Mamie's address and made sure it was correct. Then I thought about what to say and filled out the paper making certain I had spelled everything right.

Arrived Abbeville STOP
Fred surprised me in Chattanooga STOP
Ociee loves and misses you STOP

I could have written one hundred words, but I didn't want to take advantage of the nice fellow's kindness. I thanked him politely. Then I got a great idea. I'd use Papa's coins to send one to Elizabeth! She'd be extra excited about receiving her own telegram. I knew her address, too.

Miss you STOP
Feed Old Horse a carrot STOP
No bears yet STOP
Love Ociee STOP

I passed by Rebecca's but didn't take the time to visit. I noticed a new house going up around the corner. It looked to me like there were maybe three or four other ones that weren't there when I was nine.

Abbeville appeared to be growing and changing, but not as fast as Asheville. Part of me wanted Papa's town to be a big town like Asheville. More of me, however, hoped Abbeville would stay small and comfortable and remain welcoming to folks coming home.

12

Two days later, I had our house all dressed up. That done, I sat down to write a letter to my Aunt Mamie. I had to brag to her about what all I had accomplished for Papa and for the boys; and for me, too, if I were being completely honest. I yearned for that house to look more like home for the four of us.

Dear Aunt Mamie,

I miss you, but I'll be back before we both know it. Did you get my telegram? I sent it the day before yesterday, so's you would not be worried about me. I sent one to Elizabeth, too.

Did you see, Fred surprised me in Chattanooga and we rode the rest of the way together. He told some wonderful stories. I will tell them to you, but not until I can see your eyes popping out when you hear!

I have been busy making pretty Papa's house. Papa and the boys made it clean, as clean as can be, but it truly needed a girl's touch. Because you taught me good, I mean you taught me "well," I knew how to add those nice touches.

I found Mama's lace shades in an old trunk out back. When Papa got home last evening, he hung them in the parlor and in the dining room. Papa said the frilly white shades made the front windows seem as if our house were winking at him. I covered our oak dining table with a crocheted cloth and put Mama's crystal vase in the middle. Some bright yellow daffodils from a garden next door look real pretty in it, and the neighbor said there would be plenty still blooming for the wedding.

I put the quilts that your and Papa's mother made on the beds, and I placed Mama's doilies around under the oil lamps. Ben thinks they are too girlish. I told him he did not have a say. After all, a young lady is here. Oh, and the colored glass bottles; do you remember Papa's collection? Well, they are lining the kitchen windowsills. Papa was grinning ear to ear when he spotted them just sparkling in the afternoon sun.

The one thing that's missing, besides you and Mama, is flowers growing in the yard. I have a plan for that. I will tell you about it once I am done.

Tell Miss Kitty that she has a cousin. Ben has a cat named Tiger.

How are you? Have you seen Elizabeth? I will write to her next. How is Mr. Lynch? Ben says he still wants to see Aunt Mamie's snow!

Rebecca is smarter than I thought. She ironed my dress and just went on and on about how pretty it is. Thank you for making it. Rebecca said she was sorry you could not be here for their wedding. She keeps talking about the silver spoon with the "N" you sent. It must be worth all the fuss it takes for folks to get married, because they get so many presents.

If I am ever going to finish my last project, I had best get started. I will take this to the Post Office on my way.

Love to Aunt Mamie, Mr. Lynch, Old Horse, and to Miss Kitty Cat,
Your Ociee

I put my coat on over my sweater in case it got chilly later in the afternoon, slid my aunt's letter into my pocket, and saddled up Maud. So excited was I, that I near about forgot to gather my supplies! I hurried out to the shed and got Papa's shovel, a spade, and three empty feed sacks. After a quick stop at the Post Office, Maud and I headed out to our farm.

"Old girl, you know exactly where to go, don't you?" I held tight to Maud's reins. Like me, Maud knew well the way for she was heading home.

Papa mentioned that no one was living in our old house. He said the farmer who had come down from Tennessee was only interested in our land and that he had plans to build a bigger home a good piece down the road. It made me sad when Papa first told me because our house needed a family. In another way, it made me happy because I didn't want the Nashes to be replaced by anyone.

"Giddy up, Maud! Go faster, old girl!"

I reckon I was in such a hurry to get there, the way seemed longer than it really was. The horse trotted along, but not a step quicker after I kicked her. It appeared that even a Nash *horse* was determined to do things at her own speed.

Papa and Fred both mentioned having gone back to the farm a good many times, especially in the beginning. One night at dinner, Fred brought that up. "Papa, remember, we kept forgetting so many things that we'd have to ride out there, maybe two, three times a day."

"I don't know that we were as forgetful as much as we had a difficult time saying good-bye to our better days. I 'spect I kept thinking someway, somehow, I could save that farm." Papa paused, sighed, and stated, "But things generally turn out the way the good Lord plans."

Fred piped up and added, "I can tell you one thing. I'm sure more at home on a railroad track than I used to be behind a plow!"

"That's what I'm telling you, son."

I looked over at Ben. He scowled and ate a big fork piled high with mashed potatoes. Mouth full, he grumbled, "I don't give a mule's lick about going out to that old farm."

Papa reached across the table and ruffled his blond hair. "You'll want to go one of these days, Ben."

He looked at Papa with a half-irritated, half-puzzled face.

"I'll go with you," I offered.

He took another bite of food. "No, Ociee, I *am not* gonna go!"

"I am!"

Papa and Fred exchanged glances. Papa looked concerned while Fred gave me an encouraging nod.

As I got closer, I was beginning to worry that it might make me sad to see our old home. How I wished Ben had come. But the way my brother was behaving about it, he might have been more trouble than he was worth. I meant to go out there, Ben or no Ben. Furthermore, I was determined to dig up Mama's plants and to bring them back to Abbeville. We needed that part of Mama. Besides, I figured those flowers and bushes of hers must have been wondering what ever happened to their people.

The closer I got, the more the butterflies fluttered inside me. I felt about as jumpy as when our train approached the depot in Abbeville. In the distance, I could see the barn. The butterflies in my stomach were on a stampede. A few more feet up on the rise, I could just make out the outline of our house. The tin roof glistened where sun filtered through the big oak tree out front.

Maud's hoof beats on the dirt road broke the silence. Two robins flew out in front of us, their peace disturbed by our noise. We trotted up toward the front. How many times had I made this approach? My memory raced back to the last time I had been there.

I remembered looking back over Papa's shoulder and gazing at the only home I'd ever known. I was about scared to death. We were on the way to put me on the train to Aunt Mamie's. I could still feel that numbing fear. Tears clouded the image that morning. I could sense those same tears returning.

"Whoa, Maud."

I got off the horse and led her into the corral. I pulled up a bucket of water from the well and poured it into the trough for her. I gathered my things from the saddlebags, patted Maud's neck, and walked toward the house. Turning the front doorknob, I was shocked when the door swung open. Shaking, I stepped inside. The musty smell slapped me in the face.

I closed tight my eyes and wished for the past.

I wished for furniture, for kitchen smells, for laughter. I wished for a fire in the cold dark fireplace, and the welcome from my family. Mostly I wished for Mama and Papa, Fred, Ben, and me to be like we were three years ago.

I walked through the cold, empty parlor and peeked into the boys' room, into mine, then into Mama and Papa's, and finally into the kitchen. The unfurnished rooms echoed hollow under my shoes. No rugs on the wooden floors softened my steps. I sat on the floor where the table was supposed to be and I wept. Then I screamed. Then I cried again, very softly.

"Get yourself up, Ociee," I told me. I rubbed my hands together, picked up my tools, and walked out to the back porch. It hurt me to see how things had grown up so. Papa would never have let the weeds take over like that, and Mama would never have allowed the dirt and dust to claim our home.

Again, I had to push myself and be about my task. I allowed a little voice inside to urge me out into the yard. The chickens. How I used to dread having to feed those noisy, bothersome chickens every morning. I must have gone plum crazy because I was even wishing to hear those stupid chickens with all their demanding clucking and cackling.

"Gray Dog, oh my poor old Gray!" Still in mourning for that dog, it hit me hard when I spotted the places where he used to play with us. My memory's eye could still see the path where he'd follow Ben and me into the woods; the smokehouse, where he liked to curl up and sleep; the oak, always sheltering the squirrels he so longed to catch. Papa always said there'd not be a squirrel left in Marshall County, should Gray Dog ever sprout wings. I didn't even know where Gray Dog was buried.

Little wonder Ben didn't want to come with me. The sadness was eating a hole in my chest. I wanted to run away, yet I'd promised. I had promised to do this for myself and for Mama.

I caught a glimpse of her daffodils. Seemed they suddenly popped up with a warm "Howdy do, Ociee." Was it my dreaming, or were Mama's flowers bigger and brighter than those that grew next door to our in-town house?

"And hello to you!" I quickly dug up a cluster and gently placed them in one of the feed sacks. "You must want to come with me because you have so easily let go of your dirt. Don't be worried, for you'll soon be in a place where you'll be noticed."

My next attempt didn't go quite as smoothly. For what seemed like thirty minutes, I struggled to unearth a hydrangea bush. Of course, it was all sticks and would be until close to summer. Even so, I wanted to move it where it would be appreciated.

How we loved the colors of that bush! Mama's blooms sometimes grew as big as our heads. She could change their colors by having Ben or me make a wish. Perhaps I'd wish for blue. Before I knew it, Mama would present a beautiful blue blossom to me. Or Ben might make his wish for lavender. A few weeks later, Mama would call us over to the bush and say, "Look, Ben, a lavender surprise for you, my love." I remembered playing with a pink one. So pink and so big it was, I talked to the bloom as if it were a baby girl.

"Drat it all!" I fumed, as if my fussing would make the digging any easier! The hydrangea's roots had grown too deep. Nothing I could do would budge the ornery thing. I decided I'd just have to come back and try to dig it up later. Maybe Papa would help me.

I went after the hibiscus. Same problem, so I got worried then almost mad, because Mama's bushes had burrowed down too deep for me to unearth. What had Aunt Mamie said about my roots reaching to Mississippi? These dern roots went all the way to Texas!

Why were the plants so determined to stay put? Were they angry with us for leaving? I popped another clump of daffodils up and out and placed them in my sack. "You can come home with me, my yellow friends. You are far more agreeable than your brother hydrangea or sister hibiscus!"

I spotted the rosebush. Mama always kept us away from it so a thorn wouldn't prick us. I dug my shovel down deep into the soil. We'd had rain the night before; so the softened ground allowed my shovel in on the very first try.

I looked over at the hydrangea and the hibiscus. "See, I reckon your stubbornness means you two will just stay put. Goodness knows what that Tennessee man will do with the likes of you!"

As I wiggled the shovel still deeper, I urged myself on knowing that come summer, the bush would yield vivid pink blossoms. I remembered Mama cutting her roses and pumping water for the cut glass vase. She'd often whistle a tune as she arranged the bouquet. Papa claimed he could inhale that scent a good eighty feet down the road. I stood there on that cool February afternoon looking at the barren branches and could almost smell the sweet fragrance myself.

Right that minute, I vowed to return for a summertime visit. I was certain the pink rosebush was going to live. I'd go outside, cut an armful of blossoms, and fill Papa's home with familiar smells just like Mama had.

A little wren flew past my face.

I pulled the shovel up and out. Steadying my foot on the edge, I again plunged the shovel into the ground. The bush loosened.

Again and again, I pulled the shovel out, sinking it ever deeper into its surrounding soil. I was making a circle, maybe twelve or more inches from the plant itself. I was bound and determined to take enough of the Nash dirt to allow Mama's rose to feel at home.

Clunk! My shovel stopped short. I pulled it out and tried again. Cluck! The handle of the shovel hit beneath my chin. "A dern rock!"

The wren was perched nearby on the porch rail.

I moved the shovel to the other side of the bush.

The wren chirped.

Again, the soft ground gave way and Mama's bush felt the beginnings of her freedom.

A full circle was now completed around the rose; I reached my hands down deep into the dirt to lift it out. The rose wouldn't give.

"Are you gonna be stubborn like your sister hibiscus?" I complained. I stood up and went around to the side where the rock was embedded. "Reckon it's time I got you out of our way. I'm sorry, Mrs. Rose, but I'm afraid that rock has a very firm grip on your roots."

Slowly and most determinedly, I entered the shovel's blade into the ground. Twisting it, I drilled still deeper. Clunk. I rotated the shovel. Again, I hit the rock or whatever it was. I would have to dig around the thing and free the roots or the rose would never be ours.

It was beginning to get late. I knew I'd have to be back in town by the time Papa finished at the store. Fortunately, Fred wasn't around to worry about me because he'd returned to Memphis for his last run before the wedding. Ben was home from school, but that boy wasn't apt to be concerned about me. He knew I was as grown up as he was. Papa was the only person who'd fret, and I did have a little time left before he got home. I stretched out my back, gathered my strength, and plunged the shovel in for one last time. Glory be, the rock actually loosened!

I could see the little wren out of the corner of my eye.

Again, I wedged the shovel up under the rock. Oddly, the object felt somewhat lighter. Encouraged, I dug still deeper. Suddenly, the rock popped into view; and, much to my surprise, it wasn't a rock at all. It appeared to be some kind of box. I hit it with the shovel. It echoed with the then familiar "clunk." I knocked off as much of the dirt as I could.

The wren, chirping, swooped down near me.

I squatted next to the box and dusted it off with the corner of a feed sack. Metal? Yes. I wiped it cleaner. The box, perhaps six inches square, was about four inches deep and had a latch. I pried it open and looked inside.

"Good gracious sakes alive!"

My hand went to my heart.

13

The bush, its roots no longer held bound, popped up easily. I carefully placed it in a sack, and carrying the box with me, hurried to the corral to get Maud. As I led the horse back to the site, I shared my astonishing news. "You won't understand a word I'm saying, Maud, but I have to tell somebody. Look old girl, you and I have discovered treasure!"

Maud didn't respond.

I loaded the tools, the daffodils, and the rosebush into her saddlebags. Then, gripping the metal box, I attempted to mount my horse. I missed and slid down, landing on my bottom. That hadn't happened since I was a tiny girl.

Maud looked at me as if to say, "What's wrong with you?"

I put the box in the right side bag along with its longtime companion the rose bush. Stepping onto an upturned bucket, I swung up and into the saddle. Maud sensed my urgency and galloped off. I didn't even look back.

Whose box was this? How did it get in our garden? What would Papa say? Could we keep it and the contents? Maud broke into a full gallop.

Ben was going to have an absolute hissy fit. He was mad enough about having to go to school while I was home, and now he wasn't with me when I found the box. Of course, it was his own fault. If Ben hadn't been so stubborn about going to the farm, he would have been with me.

Papa was standing outside talking to a neighbor when I arrived.

"Well, good afternoon to you, young lady," he said as I dismounted. "Mr. Wiggins, this is my daughter, Ociee."

It was all I could do to respond politely. "Nice to meet you, Mr. Wiggins. But Papa, can I talk to you? Please, I must!"

He could see I needed him, so Papa excused himself from Mr.Wiggins and walked with me as I led Maud out back. I knew well to unsaddle and cool down the horse before telling Papa about what had happened.

"Ociee, I know you're up to something," he began. "What is in the saddlebags? Are those feed sacks?"

Figuring I'd forget about everything else once Papa saw the box, I showed him the flowers first. "Mama's," I grinned. "I've been to our farm." I hung the saddle on the rack and started to brush Maud.

"Well, I'll be," uttered Papa.

"We simply must have pretty flowers out front."

"Ociee, I don't know what to say. I'm very pleased that you decided to do this. I never would have thought about such a thing myself." He paused as he looked at the rosebush; the spring growth was only beginning. Papa touched my cheek. "You are your Mama's daughter, there's no question about it."

I hugged him. We embraced a second or two until Maud neighed and about scared the wits out of me. I jumped a foot.

"It's just your horse, girl. I'm afraid you've been away from the country for too long a time."

I had to laugh at myself.

"Now let's see to Maud's supper," ordered Papa. "Seems this old horse has learned to talk. Didn't you hear her telling us she's hungry?"

"You should have seen her gallop, Papa!"

"Still got it in you, huh, girl?" he said as he patted her down.

I dished out Maud's oats. "I'll ask Ben to help me plant the flowers. He's good at digging holes, and I'd need a big one for the rosebush."

"Best ask him after he's full of supper, Ociee."

"That I'll do, Papa."

Rosebush! I still hadn't told Papa about the box. I couldn't wait to get him inside and show it to him. Papa was finishing up with Maud and getting into one of his teasing moods. "Ociee girl, I believe we should cut an armful of my Bertie's roses for Fred's wedding!"

"George Nash!" I put my hands on my hips and scolded, "That wedding will be in ten days. You know good and well those roses won't bloom until next summer. Now which one of us has been away from the country too long?"

"I was only wishing, dear girl."

I was just eleven years old, but I could see the sadness cloud over Papa's face. George Nash was still grieving for his Bertie every bit as much as he did on the day she passed away. I had to wonder if any of us would ever get over her death.

"Maybe Mama's roses will bloom for us, Papa," I whispered.

He didn't answer.

I hid the box under the skirt of my coat and followed him inside. "There is one other thing. It might cheer you up, Papa."

He stopped.

"One other thing?"

"This." I handed him the box. "It was buried under Mama's rose."

Papa placed the box on the kitchen table and sat down. He opened the latch. His eyes all but popped out when he saw what was inside. "Saints preserve us, Ociee! Silver coins!"

I knelt at his feet. "Can we keep it Papa?"

Papa wanted me to tell him the exact spot where I'd found the box.

"You remember, Papa, Mama's bush was planted on the left side of the kitchen steps, not eight feet away from the well. The box was on the left side of the bush and just back of it." I explained, "It was buried so close to the house, I couldn't get around behind to dig it up."

"Hmmm." Papa lit his pipe and started to pace about.

I jumped up. "The roots crawled over toward the box. Mama's rose was trying to protect the treasure!"

Papa continued to pace. He'd sit down, look at the silver, stand up, and walk in a circle. Then he'd sit back down again, look at me, and shake his head, "I declare, I just declare!"

I followed him doing everything he did and saying, "Papa? Papa?" As much as we were wiggling around and jabbering, anybody watching would have guessed we'd stepped in a pile of angry red ants.

He sat down. "There must be close to a hundred dollars in silver!" He dumped out the contents on the table.

"One hundred dollars? Papa, we are rich!"

"Now, calm yourself, Ociee, I'm not positive."

I wanted to count the silver all by myself. Papa let me. But each time, I got a different total. "I'm a might jittery."

"I'd be glad to count it for you, dear. Mr. Fitch seems to trust me with his bookkeeping."

I let him.

"I get exactly one hundred and five dollars!"

"Yeehaw!" I shouted again and again.

"What's all the hollering?" asked Ben, breathless as he ran inside. "I could hear you two doors down."

"Look," I showed him. "I found buried treasure under one of Mama's rosebushes."

For once, Ben was dumbstruck.

We put our supper on the table, but Papa, Ben, and I weren't the least bit interested in eating. I couldn't recall another time when Ben wasn't hungry. That was certainly understandable; after all, neither my brother nor I had ever seen that much money.

"'Course Papa," I pointed out, "You keep count of money at the store every day, so this isn't all that exciting to you."

"That may be true, Ociee, but this is a different situation. I'm not exactly accustomed to having more than one hundred dollars in my kitchen! Fact is, I'll be relieved to get it out of our home first thing tomorrow. I may not sleep a wink this night." Papa poured the silver into a leather pouch and took it to a safe place until morning.

The empty box was on the table in front of Ben and me.

"Why did *you* to have find it anyway, Ociee?" grumbled Ben as he fingered the metal container. "To think, that box has been hiding there a thousand years with us walking all over it. Then, here comes Ociee Nash. She digs a hole and, boom, there it is!"

"Wasn't *that* easy, Ben."

Papa stood in the doorway. "Couldn't have been a thousand years, son. Those coins aren't even fifty years old."

"Still stinks that my sister found it. Treasure finding is a man's work."

"Shoulda gone with me," I retorted.

Ben glared. "Not fair, it's not fair at all. Besides, I was stuck in school."

"Didn't find it 'til late afternoon," I added smugly. That brought Ben to his feet.

Papa raised his voice, "Now, Ociee, Ben, that's quite enough."

We sank down into our seats.

I asked permission to get up.

"You may." I took the box over to the sink as Ben picked at his food. I dunked it into hot soapy water to let it soak for a while and sat back down to eat, too. Papa was irritated enough with our arguing, so we behaved good as gold.

"How should we spend the treasure, Ben?" I said, trying to get him away from the jealous part. I also wanted to plan the spending.

Ben perked up with that.

But Papa cleared his throat and called for our attention. "Children, you must understand something. Listen to me now. According to the law, the silver belongs to the man who purchased our farm."

"No!" I argued. "It's mine, I found it, er, it's ours anyway. Besides, that man doesn't even live there."

"As much as I wish it wasn't so, I'm afraid it would still be considered his property," explained Papa.

I was crushed flat like a beetle bug. I pushed my corn around in circles. I was mad enough at that farmer for buying our house in the first place. It appeared to me the terrible farm-stealing man from Tennessee was about to steal our silver.

Papa began one of his talks about doing things the way an honest man would.

"I'm not an honest *man*," I protested.

Papa gave me his serious look. "Ociee Nash, you know very well what I mean."

I wanted to stomp my foot, but I held back.

Ben was on my side. He said Miss Brown gave him a big thick book to read about pirates. "On some island this one pirate found a chest full of jewels, silver cups, and gold. I'm sure there were silver coins, too, just like Ociee's. Anyway, he was so happy with his treasure that he decided to stay there. He even reformed his evil ways and never attacked another ship, not ever again!"

Papa asked, "Ben, are you quite certain that's how the story went?"

"That's the idea of it, Papa. The main thing was that the pirate got to keep what he found!"

"Your sister is not a pirate, Ben, and neither are you."

My brother and I knew when not to argue with Papa. I pushed around the corn on my plate a little bit more and ate a bite or two of chicken. We had cornbread with sorghum syrup for dessert.

After dinner we left the dishes to soak. Papa wanted the three of us to sit on the porch for a spell. There'd be only a short time before the sun went down and it would be too cold out, even with a coat. We talked and waved to folks as they walked by. It was all Ben and I could do to keep from running into the street to tell everyone in town about the silver; but Papa had made it abundantly clear that we were to be quiet about it. Our Papa didn't often put his foot down; but when he did, we knew to pay attention.

As we sat in the chilly air, I wrapped my shawl up close to my face and thought what a wonderful thing it was to be a Nash. As much as I fussed about keeping the treasure, I appreciated that Papa set lofty standards for our family. In truth, I wasn't the sort of girl to claim another person's belongings.

Ben's cat jumped into my lap. "Well, hello there, Tiger. Where have you been? Are you about to get used to having Ociee in your home?" He purred as I scratched his head.

Papa reached over and stroked the cat. "Looks like you've made a friend, Ociee." He turned to Ben. "Say, boy, tell us a tale. You're good at that."

"Want to hear more about that pirate, Papa?"

"Ben."

My brother knew what that tone meant.

"Had something funny in mind, son."

"Can't think of anything to make you laugh, Papa."

I grinned. Some of Ben's best stories began with that line. I settled in to listen.

Ben was the funniest when he was trying to be serious. He wouldn't admit to it, but Ben liked being a clown. That night as we huddled in the chill, Ben talked about the lady who came to his school to teach the twelve- and thirteen-year-olds how to dance.

"In she came; she was kind of pretty, I guess. She had black curls that were pulled back in a blue bow that matched her eyes. We boys were planning to escape out the schoolhouse window. I never heard a person's voice sound so different. She musta been from Ireland or some faraway place like that."

"Poor lady," said Papa. "She was very brave to take on you bunch of rascals."

Ben nodded. "Reckon so."

I snuggled next to Papa.

"She made us line up and bow to the girls. Bow, like they were queens or something! Then we had to hold them around their middles.

That was a might embarrassing for us boys; but the girls liked it, at first anyhow."

Papa said, "Uh-oh."

Ben got to his feet. "I was glad to be so tall. My friend Stanley had to look right into Ruthie's throat; and Willard was eyeball to eyeball with his partner Lucy. She had a cold and kept sneezing in Willard's face."

"Who'd you have for a partner, Ben?" I asked.

He mumbled, "Sue Lynn. She's nice, I s'pose. Looks something like you, with hair your yellow color."

I noticed Ben turned the same shade of red as Fred. Papa saw, too, because he smiled and raised his eyebrows at me. We both chose not to tease Ben, right then anyhow.

"And then the lady's husband came in with a fiddle. He made that fiddle himself, and he could play it, too. Mr. and Mrs. Watts, they were called. She was clapping, and he was fiddling."

"All of us were bumping into one another. Stanley fell down because he couldn't see where he was going. He'd closed his eyes real tight so he didn't have to look at Ruthie. Willard copied the idea and fell down, too. He took Lucy with him. She got mad and kicked him on the knee. That made Willard mad so he hollered out, 'Lucy, you made me slip on all your sneezings.'"

Ben was twirling around the porch acting out all his classmates' antics. He became Stanley using his hand to block his eyesight as he tumbled down onto the floor. He stood up and became Lucy with a very loud "A-choo."

With the loud noise, Tiger shot from the porch and scampered down the street.

Ben didn't notice; he was too busy acting out his parts. He kicked wildly at an imaginary Willard and hurled himself down again. "All the time, Mr. Watts kept on with his fiddling."

Papa looked at me and burst out laughing. "Can't you just see that!"

Egged on, Ben began to strum an imaginary fiddle. Then he spun himself around, saying in a higher voice, "Mrs. Watts danced in circles not paying any mind to the laughing and the kicking and the falling around."

I clapped and Papa joined me.

Ben took a bow and said, "I liked the dancing lessons a whole lot more than I thought I would."

Papa and I were holding on to one another laughing so hard we couldn't catch our breaths. I still wasn't able to get out a word, but Papa wiped his eyes with his handkerchief and chuckled, "Ben Nash, that sounds like one outlandish bunch of dancing students to me. Isn't the idea to keep from falling down?"

Ben grinned. "Not for us!" He knew he was funny.

In a singsong voice I teased, "Bennie, tell us more about Sue Lynn."

"Stop it, Ociee. She's just a silly girl."

Papa joined in, "Rebecca Hutchinson started out a silly girl herself!"

"Oh dear, do I have to get used to another sister?" I giggled.

"No!" shouted Ben.

"Oh, we're both teasing you, Ben. Many a year will go by before we have another wedding in this family," said Papa. "And many, many more of your wonderful tales will yet be shared."

I hadn't noticed the coldness coming while my brother was putting on his show, but I surely noticed afterwards. "I'm cold, think I'll go inside and wash up the dishes."

Papa was pleased. "Lord have mercy, but my children are growing up! Thank you, dear girl."

I re-warmed the water with a kettleful heated on the stove and started on the utensils, plates, and glasses. At the bottom of the dishpan, I could see the box. The grime had begun to come off. Once the dishes were clean and set aside to dry, I worked on the pots, and last of all, on the nasty, sticky chicken skillet. I heard Papa coming down the hallway.

"Need my help?"

"You came inside at the perfect time, Papa." I handed him the skillet and reached down into the bottom of the dishpan to retrieve the box. My curiosity had about gotten to me.

Using the scrub brush, I was able to clean the top off pretty well. Each corner had a scrolled design, which at some point must have cascaded partway down the sides. I turned it over. There was some engraving.

"Look here, Papa!"

We tried to make out the letters. The first one was mostly gone. The second, perhaps it was a "W" or a "V" maybe. But what all but jumped out of the dirty dishwater into our faces was the last name engraved on the bottom of the metal box. As clear as if it had been written with Papa's bookkeeper's pen were spelled out the letters, N-A-S-H.

"Papa?"

14

That night I snuggled down in my bed and opened my journal. I began to write.

Today I found my very first treasure chest. It is a metal box and inside was one hundred and five dollars worth of silver coins! Best of all, OUR name Nash is carved into the back of the box! Papa has not said so as yet, but I believe we may get to keep it. Because this was the most exciting entry ever in my journal, I added the date. *February 22, 1900.*

Papa and I got up early the next morning. Not very long after breakfast, we walked into Fitch's Mercantile.

"George? I thought you were taking a free day to spend with your daughter," said a surprised Homer Fitch.

I jumped out from behind Papa. "Good morning, Mr. Fitch. Show him Papa, show him what I found!"

When Mr. Fitch saw the box of silver coins, his jaw dropped near about to the plank floor.

"And, Papa, show him the 'Nash' name on the back."

Papa scratched his head and commented, "Homer, the fact that Ociee came upon the box itself was curious enough. Now, there's the money inside. It amounts to $105. See, we have it right here."

I grinned.

"So you can imagine our shock at Ociee's cleaning it only to uncover *our* name engraved. Up until then, I figured whatever was on the property would rightfully belong to the new owner."

"So, that means the treasure belongs to us, doesn't it? Right, Papa? Mr. Fitch?"

Neither man answered.

Mr. Fitch stroked his chin whiskers. "Umm, the name on it says 'Nash,' no doubt about it. This is a baffler, George. But, as I think back about it, don't I remember that when I was a boy, there had been another Nash at your place? Had to have been a relative?"

"Yes, it's true! Tell him what you told us last night, Papa!"

Once again I heard Papa explain that a North Carolina cousin of ours had originally settled the land. He purchased it back in the early 1860s.

"In his will, Joseph Nash bequeathed this property to my father. In 1879, when Mamie and I got word that our cousin Joseph had passed away, we'd already lost Father, well, several years back. So, because the property would then have belonged to his heirs, Joseph's farm went to Father's survivors, or to Mamie and me. Knowing well that neither one of us wanted to see any Nash land go unclaimed, she and I discussed how to best honor the man's wishes.

"However, Homer, there is something else I want you to know. My beloved Bertie and I had not been married very long at that time, only since that summer; and neither she nor I knew the first thing about farming. Even so, my bride was a truly courageous woman and agreed to give up everything she'd ever known to travel out west with the likes of me. Together, she and I would work that farm and raise our three children." He looked at me to make certain I'd heard what he had said.

I glowed with pride.

"This is quite a story, George, but now, what are you going to do about all this money?" He indicated the box. "Perhaps you and I had better take a seat and talk." Mr. Fitch asked, "Ociee, would you mind going back there after my wife? Ask Mrs. Fitch, if she could, to come out and watch the counter for me. Please tell her that George Nash and I have important business to see about."

"Yes, sir." I hurried back to their quarters and knocked. Mrs. Fitch nodded yes, quickly fastened her apron, and came out.

"How are you this morning, Ociee?" she asked walking into the store. "And you, George?"

"You cannot imagine how fine we are!"

She eyed me with a puzzled look.

As she poured the men hot coffee, Mrs. Fitch asked, "Dear child, would you like something to drink, too?"

"No thank you, ma'am." I was much too excited to put a drop more of anything into my body before I found out if we were keeping the silver.

The two men sat in rocking chairs, propping their feet up on the potbellied stove. I wandered around the store looking at first one thing then the next. I thought of Aunt Mamie as I fingered through the spools of thread. I'd best be writing to her about the buried treasure and to Elizabeth, too. That girl was going to have my head, because I hadn't yet answered her letter to Abbeville. I'd do it that very afternoon and tell her our news.

Of course, I was listening with both ears as the men talked. I always loved to hear Papa telling any story, but this one was extra special.

I waited for Mrs. Fitch to finish with a customer.

"Thank you, so much, Miss Melanie." She carefully marked down the total in the customer's account. "I do hope your new dress will turn out well."

I was again reminded of Aunt Mamie, and thought to myself what a beautiful dress she would have made from that lavender flowered fabric. I didn't say anything about it, of course. I just thought what I wanted to think.

"Mrs. Fitch, do you want to know our secret?"

As I let her in on it, she grew as excited as I. "Isn't it a wonder that when Mama planted that rose, she didn't find that box herself?"

"It was not yet the good Lord's time, my dear," said Mrs. Fitch in a matter-of-fact manner.

"I'll try to explain the Lord's timing part to Ben Nash. He's mad I made the discovery instead of him, but I trust my brother wouldn't question the Lord's schedule."

"Deary me, I should hope not."

Mrs. Fitch had been a good friend of Mama's, so I decided to tell her about the wren. "It was a curious thing, ma'am. There was this little bird flying around in the back of our old house. A tiny brown wren. I've never noticed one quite as friendly. Truthfully, that wren was encouraging me to keep on digging!"

"Ociee, child, don't you see? That treasure was found at the perfect moment, just in time for your brother's wedding. And it was to be you, not anyone but you, who came upon it. I wouldn't be a bit surprised if your sweet Mama wasn't told about that box by someone at her home on high. That bird may have been an angel in disguise."

"Oh, Mrs. Fitch, you really believe that?"

"You can be certain of one thing. If I knew Bertie Nash, she wasn't about to miss out on what's going on with her family, her firstborn's wedding especially. Likely, Ociee, it was Bertie Nash who whispered in your ear to go and get her flowers in the first place."

My heart took a leap.

Papa sipped his coffee. "Homer, I am sure you know that the Yankees came down through Holly Springs and Waterford on their way over to Vicksburg?"

"Hell, yes, I do!" He caught a glimpse of his wife and me and hesitated. "You must excuse me, ladies. I just get so dern mad when I think about the damage those blue devils did around these parts!" growled Mr. Fitch. "I was just a young boy during the War, but I've heard those terrible tales my whole life!"

"Even so, Homer, watch your tongue!" scolded his wife, indicating me.

I shuddered. I never could imagine folks shooting at other folks anywhere in our rolling green hills of Marshall County. I could hardly abide it when my brothers shot a squirrel. Fact was, I never did understand how or why good people could get into all that fighting. Papa often said not many people were as tolerant as his Ociee. I wasn't quite sure what "tolerant" meant, so I asked. Papa explained that it was liking folks and wanting all that was best for them. His words made me proud to be considered a tolerant person. I'd decide later if that were too prideful before I added it to my journal.

Papa turned back to Mr. Fitch. "Now we must understand that everybody got into a terrible panic when they heard, 'The Yankees are coming!'"

"Indeed," agreed Homer, balling his hands into fists and setting his jaw so his teeth clinched.

I got a chill at hearing his words. I walked over near Papa and squatted down close at his side. I looked into his soft eyes. "You would have kept those soldiers from fighting on our place, wouldn't you, Papa?"

He cupped my chin in his hand.

"I'd have tried my best." Papa winked at me. He went on, "As we know, people were out of their minds with fear. Many simply had to pick up and abandon their homeplaces. They might not have had an hour to prepare and no way to carry all their belongings with them. Also there was the worry of being robbed, captured, or even killed along the way."

"How terrible!" I said.

Papa patted my head to soothe me. Then he continued, "The thing to remember is that oftentimes, as they were leaving, folks would quickly try to bury their valuables with every intention of coming back for them once the soldiers were gone."

"Valuables, Papa?"

"Jewelry, family pieces, sets of sterling, fine glass, gold, money, just about anything of value."

"Silver coins?"

"Yes, Ociee, and they would most certainly bury silver coins."

"I just knew it!"

Papa nodded to me and continued, "I've come to the conclusion that the Yankee soldiers were close by, so Joseph Nash buried the silver in this box. However, in his haste to get away, the fellow either failed to mark the spot well; or perhaps, he simply never had need of it."

I jumped up, and holding out my the palms of my hands, I announced, "So, years and years had passed, and here I came. I was only trying to dig up a rosebush, and I found Cousin Joseph's buried treasure!"

"In all my days, I just never heard of such an incredible piece of luck," said Mr. Fitch.

"A gift from Bertie Nash, if you ask my opinion," offered Mrs. Fitch.

I looked at her and grinned. Papa was watching, too. "Adelaide, are you filling my daughter's head full with your angels again?"

"George, you know I am."

Papa nodded. "That's fine with me."

He turned to Mr. Fitch. "So, Homer, what are your thoughts about the money? Do you believe it rightfully belongs to us?"

"George, that money definitely belongs to the Nashes. In my mind, there's no question about it."

"Hooray!" I shouted.

Papa turned to me. "So, Miss Ociee, what do you think about that? It appears you've stuck gold."

"Silver, Papa, I struck silver!"

15

I wrote to Aunt Mamie and to Elizabeth as soon as I got home. I was writing so fast, I could hardly read my own handwriting. That Aunt Mamie and my best friend would be able to understand the wonderful news was a concern; nevertheless, I couldn't slow my shaking fingers!

I found a treasure! I began.

I penned the letters side by side, a line on one, a line on the other. In Elizabeth's, as soon as I told her about the silver, I thanked her for writing to me. I also put her mind to ease saying I'd still not seen the first bear and not even my gypsy man, although I was actually pretty disappointed about not seeing him. I mentioned that I was glad she was making A's in school and to tell the other children hello from Ociee, and that I truly missed playing in last week's surprise snowfall. I knew she'd be getting mighty fussy about my neglecting her. So, at the end, I wrote carefully:

I have had TOO MUCH to do to get our house and these men folks ready for the wedding. But I still think about you every day. Guess what? I'm going to buy you a present with my silver. I will buy it as soon as I get to Asheville.

With love, your caring but too busy best friend, Ociee

In Aunt Mamie's, I told all about digging up the rosebush. When she came for Mama's funeral, my aunt cut roses from that very bush.

Aunt Mamie, you were just inches away from finding the treasure yourself.

I could hardly wait for her to read those words. I wished I could have seen her face when she did. Naturally, I mentioned the Joseph Nash box and how my Papa figured out its mystery.

I'd hoped to hear back from her before I traveled back to Asheville. However, it seems Papa had his own surprise for me. Later, he told me that he had wired his sister as soon as I left Fitch's. Because of that, Aunt Mamie and Mr. Lynch turned right around and sent a telegram to congratulate me. It came just two days later. I was glad they would get all the details from me.

Their telegram read:

Hats off to Ociee STOP
Spend silver wisely STOP
Love from Aunt Mamie, Mr. Lynch and Old Horse STOP

I believed that I was the only person who had ever gotten a telegraph message from a horse.

Fred's wedding was six days away. That night I sat down with Papa.

"Papa, I've been thinking about the $105. Reckon as how I should do something with it."

"Mr. Fitch is happy to hold it in his safe for you until you decide. What is it you're thinking of doing?"

"That's just it, Papa. It's not my money; it's the Nashes' money. It even said so on the box. I 'spect I should share it with the family."

Papa cocked his head and settled in to listen to me.

I showed him my writing tablet. I'd divided the $105 by five figuring one portion for Papa, one for me, one for Ben, and one for Aunt Mamie; and I asked the one important question that had troubled me about my plan. "Papa, do I have to give Fred two shares? Since there's two of them, do I have to share twice? Oh, Papa, please say I don't have to. I can't divide it out even by six."

"Ociee, it's yours to decide; you can do it any way you like, but I think one share would be a gracious plenty for Fred and Rebecca. They would be most grateful about your generosity, I'm quite sure."

"Whew!"

"But, darlin' girl, I don't want you to include me in your figuring. I am a rich man without your silver; I'm rich because you are your Papa's treasure."

"But Papa I want most for you to have it!"

"Good, then it's mine to give, and I choose to give it to you, my dear daughter."

I'd simply give it right back to Papa, I decided.

The next day, I asked Mrs. Fitch to sell me three sheets of wrapping paper. To keep my secret, I was careful to shop while Papa was in the office with the books. When Mrs. Fitch understood what I was going to do, she generously gave me the paper, along with some pretty ribbon and three boxes. I thanked her, hurried home and spent the next hour fixing up my surprises. In each box, I counted out twenty-one dollars in silver coins and wrote a note to the person it was for:

To Ben, this is to be used only for your dreams. Better not waste it!

To Papa, I am sorry, but I just cannot help giving this to you.

To Rebecca and Fred, please spend this on something special, because it is a gift from me, and from Mama.

In the box for my brother and his bride, I added a lace handkerchief that was our Mama's. I spread it open and put in some sweet-smelling sachet. Then I tied the hankie in a knot. Papa's was just plain because I figured I'd have a hard enough time talking him into keeping it, let alone accepting the present inside. In Ben's box, I added some pebbles from the schoolyard. He was one to shake his presents, and those rocks would surely confuse him!

I planned to give Aunt Mamie hers in person when I went home the middle of March. I couldn't imagine how thrilled she'd be. The thought of her excited face was going to make my leaving Abbeville not quite so difficult. At any rate, I hoped that was true.

The first package I delivered was to Rebecca. When I knocked on the door, Mrs. Hutchinson answered. I hid the box behind my back.

Rebecca's mother looked almost exactly like her, but her brown hair had gray streaks in it. Also, instead of hanging down and tied back in a bow, Mrs. Hutchinson's hair was twisted in all sorts of directions that came together in a knot on the top of her head. Still, the rounded shape of her chin and tiny button nose could have as easily been those of Fred's sweetheart.

"Ociee, how charming of you to drop by. Do come in."

I'd been to the house before but it never failed to amaze me how fine a home it was. It was as nice as any in Asheville. Inside was rich folk's furniture. In the living room, there were three matching pieces with curved arms and legs cut from dark polished wood. The furniture was covered in deep blue velvet. As I sat in one, I felt as if I were sitting on a royal throne.

While I waited for Rebecca to come downstairs, I looked up at the ceiling. It was too high for me to touch, even if I'd been rude enough to stand on the table. I gazed around the room and noticed crystal candleholders on either side of the settee. The walls were covered in floral paper that reminded me of my aunt's house. I got up to better see the paintings of Rebecca's relatives. At least, I assumed the people were her relatives. Truthfully, neither of the ladies on the wall was as pretty as my new sister.

She came in with her mother. "What a nice surprise, Ociee." Rebecca gave me a kiss on my cheek.

"I've got another surprise for you." With that, I handed her the box.

"Thank you!"

"I wanted to give it to you and Fred at the same time, but since he can't get here until just before your wedding, I decided to bring it for you today. Fred will find out soon enough."

"Well, let's see what have we here." She carefully unwrapped my gift.

Why girls did this, I might be able to understand when I got older; but for the life of me, it remained a puzzle that day. Rebecca was so preoccupied admiring the hankie that held the money, she didn't even notice what was inside. That turned out to be a good thing, however, because soon she would need the hankie to blow her nose. My wedding present was supposed to please her, but it had only made her cry! It made her mother cry, as well.

"Did I do something wrong?"

"Oh, no, Ociee, it's, it's just that your message mentioning your mama is so dear." She started to cry again.

I shrugged my shoulders.

Mrs. Hutchinson put her arms around me and gushed, "What a precious thing you are, dear, dear little one!"

I was already getting nervous enough with their weeping and the to-do about my present, but it got even worse. When Rebecca finally got to the coins, the poor thing all but collapsed smack dab in the middle of the fancy parlor.

Mrs. Hutchinson gurgled, patting fast her chest, "You dear thing, you! Our Rebecca is most fortunate to be marrying this fine young man, Fred Nash, who has such a darling sister!"

Mr. Hutchinson walked into the room. "Look who's here, dear, it's little Ociee Nash."

I fumbled around but managed to excuse myself, saying I had some things to do for Papa. I couldn't take any more of that high-spirited carrying on, especially from Mrs. Hutchinson.

"Ben! You're already home from school?" Actually, I was missing my own school and was lonesome for Miss Small and my classmates. It wasn't nearly as much fun for me to do my lessons without sharing it with them. "Sure feels strange for me not to be at my school."

"I wish I was you," he complained as he cut a slice of cake. "You want a piece, Ociee?"

"Please. How did your arithmetic test turn out?" After I asked him that, I felt more like Ben's Mama, instead of his younger sister. I poured us some milk.

"Mighty fine, least I hope so. Say, I did get a good grade on my story. See right here, Ociee, I got a 'B+' on it."

"What's your story about?"

"You can read it if you want, but I'll tell you first. It's about a boy who buys a mule and goes out to California to search for a gold mine. He spends five whole years prospecting all over those mountains. The Rocky Mountains they're called. I looked that up so's to be right.

"Finally, when he is a grown man, 'bout Fred's age, he is almost ready to give up. Suddenly, one morning, the man, oh, by the way, I named him Benjamin, is chipping away down deep in his mine."

I smiled at the Benjamin part.

"Guess what? He finds the most gold that any body else has ever found! Benjamin buys one thousand acres of land and starts himself a farm. He sets aside a big space for his mule to thank him, you know. The farm's got a creek and a shade tree and lots of grass for the mule to eat. And she can run as she pleases. And, here's the best part, Benjamin has his pickaxe coated with gold and hangs it in his house over his stone fireplace. You can see why Miss Brown thought I deserved a B+, can't you?"

"Yes, I can," I said. "Did you name the mule 'Maud'?"

"No, why would I do that?"

I thought about my gift for him. "Wait here, Ben, and don't you move." I went back to my room and reached under the bed to retrieve his box. Going back into the kitchen I was surprised to find that my brother was actually waiting for me, and he was even being patient about it.

"It's not a gold pickaxe, but maybe you'll like it," I announced as I handed him the present.

He began to shake the box. The rocks rattled against the clinking coins.

I knew Ben pretty well.

"Sounds like it has rocks in it, brass buttons, too?" Ben's eyebrows furrowed.

"You're right. The rocks are from your schoolyard. You know, Ben, where you just got your B+."

My brother tore open the paper. He looked inside. "Ociee? What in the world?"

"It's for you, Ben. See, read the note."

"Only for my dreams? My dream is to find that gold mine! Do you think this could buy me that mule?"

"A mule?"

Right away, I questioned what I'd done in giving Ben Nash twenty-one dollars. I felt like I'd just kicked open a beaver dam. Leaves and sticks and stones were scattering everywhere, and all the water was gushing out.

"Ben! Please, talk with Papa. He'll be home in two hours."

He heard the "Papa" part, but he missed the warning in my voice. I hoped he wouldn't leave that very minute.

"Stay put, Ben! Wait for Papa."

"You're right, Ociee, Papa will know where we can buy the best mule!"

"It's not about a mule, Ben," I twisted my hands together. "You can't be taking off and going to California. We'd be so worried about you."

"You went to North Carolina."

"That was a different thing."

"Not true, it was only a different direction."

"Besides, Aunt Mamie was waiting on the other end of my trip."

Still louder, Ben shouted, "I'll have a mule with me."

I got so mad and upset, I started to scream. My brother patted my hand and looked right in my face. "Don't get upset, Ociee. I wouldn't be leaving until after Fred's wedding."

16

Sure enough, Papa got home and managed to get Ben's mind off that mule.

"Boy, it will take months to ride all the way to the Pacific Ocean on the back of even the fastest mule you could find. Best be talking to Fred about going west on one of his trains."

With that, Ben raced out of the house. He meant to find his brother as soon as he could. I wondered if he'd run all the way to Memphis.

Papa spotted his gift, turned and looked at me. "Darling girl, I know you mean to please me, but your Papa can't be taking this generous gift from you. How about we put it in the bank and keep it there for something special, your own marriage someday. This silver would come in handy for such as that."

"My wedding? Papa, I could never leave you, not forever like that!"

"You may change your mind, young lady."

I nodded and sort of smirked. This was one time my Papa was wrong as could be.

By Saturday, Ben's passion for prospecting was put aside as he fumbled to button his collar. "Dern it all, I can't hardly stand this tight thing!"

The four of us were all running about crashing into one another and yelling as we frantically tried to get ready for the wedding. Tiger scampered from room to room, hiding under one bed then the next. I suspected that poor cat worried just what would happen next. I was feeling the same way; it occurred to me to hide under a bed, too.

"One mirror does just fine on a regular day," grumbled Papa. "Come here, Ben, let me do that for you."

My hair was a mess with curls going every which way, so I decided to tie it back with pink ribbon. Mama must have been guiding my hands because I managed to get every piece in the bow the first time around. I pinched my cheeks to make them rosy like Rebecca had showed me.

I slipped the dress over my head. Aunt Mamie had sewn it so beautifully, and Rebecca ironed it perfectly. I surely didn't want to muss it up putting it on. I tied the sash and spun around making the skirt flow like rose petals in a breeze. I took my turn admiring myself in Mama's mirror. I looked over my shoulder, turned again, and admired myself full front. I did look like the princess Papa said I was. It wasn't bragging; it was simply the truth.

"Papa, do I look all right?"

He put his hand over his heart. "My lady, Miss Ociee Nash, may I have this dance?"

"Dance?" I giggled. "Don't throw me on the floor like Willard did Lucy!"

"Never, my lady!" Papa took me in his arms and whirled me around the room like I was the belle of the ball. He held out his arms and, holding my hands in his, looked me over from toe to top. I saw his eyes twinkle. "Darling girl, you are every bit as lovely as your Mama on that day I first saw her."

He touched the locket and his lips brushed my forehead.

"Papa!" yelled Ben. "Somebody stole my dag nabit sock!" When my brother looked at me, his mouth dropped open. "Gosh, Ociee, You look right nice."

"Thank you."

"Doesn't she!" agreed Papa. He reached down on the floor. "This sock, son? Appears the thief brought it back. If you'll just quit your fussing, we can get you to look as handsome as your sister looks pretty."

At that moment, Fred came running in from the backyard. "I think I'm sick."

"Oh, Fred, no, that's just terrible," I moaned.

"What's wrong, son?" asked Papa.

"My stomach's all queasy-like, and my head is pounding, and my knees are shaking so that I can't stand in one place."

Papa signed, and then he let out with a great big laugh. "Fred Nash, I suffered the same sickness on my own wedding day. I believe every bridegroom there ever was has experienced those before ceremony jitters. That's all that's ailing you, my boy."

The two of them went out on the front porch.

"I ain't never gonna get married," said Ben.

I corrected him, "Ben, don't you be saying 'ain't.' It's not good English."

"I don't care how you put it, Ociee. No girl is ever gonna get me into this fix."

"Not even Sue Lynn?"

Ben made an ugly face. He didn't dare do anything else, or we'd both mess up our clothes.

"Come on Ociee, Ben! Your brother has recovered. It's time we left for church."

It was a perfect March morning. The sun was out, and I could feel the warmth through the stained-glass windows of the Hutchinsons' church. I was glad it wasn't our church, because I didn't want to think about Mama's funeral during Fred's wedding. I only wanted to think of our Mama looking down on our family from her glory.

It surprised me to find so many folks already in their pews. I scurried to get us a good seat, but Papa stopped me. "Dearest, they have special places set aside for us. Besides, you have your bridesmaid responsibility to think about." He pointed to a door in the back of the church. "Ociee, it's time for you to see to Rebecca. We'll find her in there."

I had nearly forgotten I had a job to do. Aunt Mamie had explained it, and so had Rebecca, and Papa, too. But I'd gotten too caught up in how pretty I looked that day. Mostly, I wanted to show off.

Papa took my hand and knocked on the door. "Got your bridesmaid here." He grinned proudly at me.

He glanced in and caught a glimpse of Fred's bride. "Good gracious, Rebecca, but you are a gorgeous young lady!"

"Oh, Mr. Nash, thank you," said Rebecca, giving Papa a kiss.

"I should warn you, my son may burst with pride when he sees you!"

When I looked at Rebecca, I could have fallen over from the shock. Fred's sweetheart was beautiful, more beautiful than I'd ever dreamed she'd be. She wore a floor-length white lace gown. The soft lace began at the top of her neck, covered her arms to the center of her hands, and fell into a train that trailed four feet behind her when she walked. So soft was her gown to feel, it could have been a baby's dress. Atop her head circled a wreath of tiny yellow flowers; her brown curls cascaded over her shoulders and down her back. Her face glowed.

Rebecca's first words to me were, "Ociee, you look exquisite!"

I ran over and hugged her. Why I cried, I'll never understand. It must have been one of those times I was too happy to do much else.

Mrs. Hutchinson also commented on how nice I looked, so I bragged about my aunt's sewing. I finally got my mouth working right and attempted to tell Rebecca how pretty she was. "It's not that you aren't always pretty. It's that today you look like a queen or an angel or something extra special! Your gown is about the most gorgeous thing I nearly ever saw, and your hair, well, I love that you have flowers in it."

"Mother made the wreath." Mrs. Hutchinson looked on pleased as she could be with her success.

"Fred's already nervous; he's gonna faint when he sees you!"

"I hope not!" said Rebecca, looking not worried but amused.

A gentle knock came at the door. All three of us jumped. "Ready?" said the voice of a lady from their church.

"Mother!" gasped Rebecca as she turned as white as her wedding dress. Maybe Ben was right and nobody should get married. Seemed to be mighty hard on folks' nerves.

"Gather yourself, dear, this is your day. Your father will escort you. Hold your head up, smile, and enjoy every minute!" She kissed her on the cheek. "I love you." She walked into the back of the sanctuary.

The music began. Mr. Watts played his fiddle. I believe he called it a "violin" for the occasion. He didn't play gay dancing music; it sounded more high-toned than that. I had a feeling the Vanderbilts would recognize the tunes.

The lady called for me. I had to go to the bathroom, but that would have to wait. I stepped through the door clutching the flowers she handed me. I smiled nicely, held my shoulders back, and tried to walk down the aisle without stumbling. Papa winked at me, and Ben giggled. I spotted the Fitches, Miss Brown, Mr. and Mrs. Hall, Miss Ethel, Mrs. Watts, and a good many other friends from Abbeville. There was also a sea of strangers' faces. Fred told us folks were coming all the way from Memphis.

Ben's friend Willard wrinkled up his nose at me, but his mother elbowed him so he'd stop. I surely hoped Ben would notice Miss Brown and be on his best behavior for fear his teacher would get after him.

I made it safely to the front, turned, and stood next to Papa and Fred. I looked down at Fred. His britches' legs were shaking he was trembling so. The door opened and out came Mr. Hutchinson. How handsome he looked with his wavy white hair. Rebecca stepped out and took his arm. The whole room of people, had to be seventy or more, stood and turned toward them. I thought Fred would actually keel over.

His eyes about popped from their sockets as he exclaimed, "Glory be, girl!"

Some people laughed. Papa and I did.

Rebecca walked real slowly as all the church full of people "oohed and ahhed."

Fred's pants flapped as much as if he were standing in a tornado.

Her father placed Rebecca's hand in Fred's. My brother swallowed a gulp of air. A shaky "I do" was his answer when the preacher asked if he would. Seemed to me, Rebecca's answer was made with more enthusiasm than my brother's. It must be frightening to agree to take care of a person forever. I was proud of him for taking on such a big task.

After the promising part, Mr. Watts again played his violin. We all sang some hymns. I most liked "Amazing Grace." I knew all of the words, which was good, because everyone was watching to see. Also I had to hold two bouquets, the bride's and mine; I couldn't be hanging on to a songbook at the same time.

"I give you Mr. and Mrs. Fred Nash!" announced the preacher.

Everyone clapped. I'd never heard folks clap in church before. Ben put two fingers in his mouth and whistled. Papa made him quit. Afterwards, we all went over to the preacher's home, where we got to enjoy many good things to eat without having to dance!

Miss May, our family's dear old friend from out in the country, made the wedding cake. She didn't attend the ceremony. Instead, she stayed at the preacher's and stood guard over her creation. Miss May was as particular about her baking as Aunt Mamie was with her dressmaking.

"Miss May, you have outdone yourself," praised Papa.

"My pleasure, George. You know, I love these children like they belong to me."

Fred came in pulling Rebecca along. Everybody wanted to talk with the bride and groom, but my brother made a beeline for us. Fred shook Papa's hand and hugged me tight, then we swapped and Rebecca kissed us both.

"Ociee, you are just about as pretty as my new wife," said Fred. Rebecca blushed. Must have been her hearing the word "wife" and realizing she was one.

"And you're as handsome as Papa." I meant it, too.

"Miss May, Rebecca agrees with me. This wouldn't have been a perfect wedding without your cake. Thank you, we can't wait to taste it."

Rebecca added, "Yes, indeed, but it's almost too pretty to eat."

A tear ran down her face. "God bless you, darlin' children."

"Where's Ben?" asked Fred.

"Where do you think he is, son? First in line for cake, of course!"

"Excuse me," I said, hurrying across the room, "I'm second!"

"Whoa, little Nashes, you have to wait for us!" said Fred as he and Rebecca made their way through the crowd of well-wishers. Papa picked up a cup of punch and called everyone together.

"My family and I want to thank the Hutchinsons for hosting such a beautiful wedding." He raised his cup and said, "We appreciate everyone here for celebrating with us on this joyous day."

With that, Papa turned to Fred and Rebecca and said, "I salute my most fortunate son and his lovely bride. Rebecca, I do welcome you and your mother and father to the Nash family."

Papa was the "Best Man," and I delighted that everyone else at the party recognized that.

"This wedding stuff isn't as bad as I thought it'd be," said Ben.

"Who told you so?" I twirled around. I liked to watch my skirt billow.

"Musta been you, Ociee. Think we could get another piece of cake?"

"In a minute, Ben. We have to wait for others to get theirs."

Mr. Watts walked about playing his music. Folks were eating and talking. The Hutchinsons had a bunch of friends I'd never seen before. I overheard a person say one couple came from way up north. I was missing Aunt Mamie something terrible.

"I can't unloose this collar now, Ociee?" pleaded Ben.

"Better ask Papa."

Rebecca was talking to some of the guests. Fred excused himself and came over my way. "This is a happy time for me, Ociee, but a sad one, too."

"What?"

"Rebecca and I will be leaving this afternoon," he began.

I put my fingers in my ears. I knew he was going to Memphis, but I didn't want to hear him say it.

He pulled my finger away and whispered a secret. "Got something for you to ponder, Ociee. Perhaps you might think about coming to Memphis one of these days?"

"To visit? Just like Ben did! I'd like that, Fred."

He grinned. "Thought you might. I know you're quite a traveler now. Mind you, the trip would be a long one, about as many hours as it is from Asheville to Abbeville."

"Oh, Fred, I wouldn't mind that one bit. But don't you forget, you promised to visit us at Aunt Mamie's."

"I'll keep my promises, Ociee. You have my word." With that he gave me a kiss.

I hugged him tight and drank some more punch. I spotted Ben across the room. He was fussing to Papa about his collar.

Later on in the afternoon, we saw Fred and Rebecca off. Mrs. Hutchinson was near hysterical as the train pulled away. Mr. Hutchinson kept patting her shoulder over and over again and saying, "It's going to be all right, my sweet."

I went to her and tugged at her dress. "I'm sorry you're so sad."

"Thank you, my dear," she wailed.

"You're gonna be happy again. You'll see. Rebecca will come home for a visit."

Mrs. Hutchinson grabbed me and squeezed me so tight, I thought I'd break in two. I let her hang on to me as long as she wanted. I surely understood how awful she felt. Mr. Hutchinson peeled the poor, sobbing lady off of me and walked her to their buggy.

Papa, Ben, and I stopped in to see Mr. Hall and to buy my ticket for Asheville. He commented about how nice he thought the wedding was. He added, "And what a handsome family you are."

"We quite agree, sir!" said Papa. I held wide my skirt and made a curtsey.

Ben had all he could take. "Please, Papa," he begged, "now can we go home so I can get out of these clothes?"

I kept my dress on for the whole rest of the day.

17

Monday, Miss Brown told Ben he was doing so well in school that she was giving him three days off to spend time with me.

"Ben, I think your teacher's giving you a prize because you did her proud at the wedding."

"I don't need to know why, Ociee; I'm just happy to stay home."

The two of us ripped and ran up and down every hill in Marshall County. We went fishing, and we rode Maud until the poor tired horse about dropped. The first night we told Papa where we'd been and what we'd done. In truth, we told him *almost* everything.

On Wednesday morning, Miss May brought us a yummy gooey, crispy-crusted chess pie. As always, Papa told her it was the best pie she had ever baked for us.

"You can't be telling that right, George. Because, if each pie is the 'best ever,' as you insist; it must be true that the ones I baked for you years ago were terrible. No dessert can continue to improve for years on end."

"It's a mystery to me, May, but yours do!"

He asked her to join us for a piece, but she said she had to be on her way.

"Ociee, Ben," Papa said slyly, "I don't want to waste this fresh baked pie. What do you say we eat a bite this minute?"

I was amazed because we always were made to save our desserts for after supper. Our Papa had actually changed one of his rules. We three ate more than half that pie. Needless to say, Ben and I didn't have much appetite for that night's soup and cornbread. We didn't mind one bit. That pie *was* the best Miss May ever baked.

The next morning, I got up my courage and said, "Ben, let's you and me go out to the farm."

"What for? You already found the silver." Then he pondered a spell, came after me, and said, "Reckon I'll go with you, Ociee. 'Cause if I don't, you'll keep on fussing at me about it."

I didn't take time to saddle up Maud. I was afraid Ben might change his mind. I put the bit in her mouth and adjusted the reins. Ben and I climbed on from the back fence and headed out.

Ben was quiet for Ben.

As the barn and the house came into view, I could feel him tensing up. He held tightly to my waist. "This is a waste of a perfectly good day, Ociee," he grumbled. "Let's go fishing."

"No, sir, we're here now. Who knows, maybe there's more treasure?"

That got his mind working on something besides being anxious. The first thing we did was to run out back to see the hole where I'd found the box.

"Dag nabit! I wish I'd brought a shovel."

"Or a gold-coated pickaxe?" I teased. "Come on, let's take a look in the barn for something to dig with."

There was no shovel, but we did have fun poking around. Ben picked up a handful of old nails to keep.

"I keep thinking Gray Dog will run out wagging his tail and jumping in circles," Ben said. "I miss that old dog."

"Me, too."

"Tiger's fun sometimes, but a dog's better," he complained.

"Get you one, Ben."

"Maybe I will, one exactly like Gray Dog!"

"There won't ever be one like him," I said.

"You're right about that, Ociee. He was the best dog there ever was. Think I could teach Tiger to fetch?"

"Ben, I know if anyone could teach a cat to fetch, it'd be you!"

We climbed up into the hayloft. Before long, we were jumping from the loft down into a pile of old hay and leaves we'd pitched together. Both of us were laughing and rolling. For a few minutes, we were the Nash children getting into devilment. The difference was no Mama or Papa called out to stop us and to keep us from getting hurt.

We pulled up a bucket of water from Papa's well and drank our fill from the dipper. "Best water in Marshall County," I announced.

"Best water in the whole world," Ben parroted Papa.

We sat down on the porch steps and looked out into the field. Soon, the farmer from Tennessee would have his people planting the summer's crops. Much of the field had already been plowed.

"I don't miss the farming so much as I miss the being us," confessed my brother.

"Me, neither."

"I don't 'spect there's any more silver buried around here, Ociee, do you?"

"I don't know. Likely not. Say, brother, I thought you were gonna search for gold?"

"Nah, I was just talking was all. I'm always looking out for something else that makes my heart pound and my bones jiggle."

"Would you be a railroad man like Fred?"

"Nope, I kind of want to be famous instead."

"Famous!" I rolled backwards and kicked my feet on the dirt floor. Then I stood up and gestured my hand his way, "Ladies and gentlemen, I give you the world famous Ben-ja-min Nash!"

"I'll just have to show you, smarty pants!"

"You better do it, too. And when you are famous, you can come and visit me in Asheville. I will introduce you to everyone I know. Ben, I'd do that anyway, if you'd just come." I got serious then and pleaded with my brother. "Why don't you? In fact, come with me when I leave next week."

We both knew that wasn't going to happen. He had his school, and Papa would likely grieve himself to death what with Fred just marrying.

"Come on, Ben, let's go inside. Don't you want to see our house?"

Ben kicked the dirt around the bottom step. "Reckon I just don't want to," he said kind of quiet like.

"Why not?"

"Just don't."

We sat there for a while longer. Again, I asked.

Ben argued, "I came out here with you and we didn't even look for treasure. Ociee, I don't want to see inside. I want my memory to be our house with things in it and people, too. I want to close my eyes and see you, Fred, Papa, and Mama sitting around the table eating supper. I don't want to think of it empty."

He got up and stomped out to the smokehouse. Turning around, Ben called to me, "Come on, girl, and let's go see what else we can find."

Maybe Ben was right and I was wrong to go inside. Yet, seeing it had given me a good feeling. When I was inside, I was able to shut my eyes and put everything and everyone back in its place. It seemed my brother's eyes were more interested in what was going to happen down his road than from where he'd come.

I skipped a step and hurried to catch up with him.

The remainder of the afternoon, we played as we had when we were five to ten years old. We played stickball with pinecones; we terrorized squirrels and chipmunks and hid from one another. We also jumped out and scared each other. Together he and I explored every inch of our land. I told Ben the land would remain ours forever, no matter who farmed the fields.

Fortunately, I'd thought to gather together some things for us to eat as we'd left Papa's house. Ben and I sat down under the oak in the front yard and ate a chicken leg and the last of Miss May's pie. We washed down our picnic with shared ladles full of water from Papa's well.

As I licked the last of sweet pie from my fingertips, I asked, "Did you ever hear anything more about the gypsy?"

"Not anything else about *your* gypsy," he answered. "Just 'cuz you were clumsy and fell down and lost Mama's locket, you got to be his friend. And then, by dern, you were the one who got a picture of her. And that was 'cuz you got to go to Aunt Mamie's. It's not fair, Ociee!"

"I'm sorry, Ben." I really was, too.

"Reckon you should be. The gypsy must have told some of his friends about this area, though, because we've had several families of them through here this past year. Say, what was his name anyway?"

"I never asked."

"I would have," he snapped.

"I know."

Ben complained, " Papa won't let me go anywhere near the gypsy camps, says I'd be a bother. Did you ever wonder why your gypsy didn't travel with his family?"

"My gypsy had a broken heart, Ben, I just know it. I've imagined all kinds of things about him. I've wondered that he might have been shunned for doing something he didn't mean to do. Was he so sad about something that had happened, or so distressed about someone he lost that he couldn't bear being around the other gypsies? I could tell it by the look in his eyes. I don't suppose I'll ever know; but, to this minute, I find myself wishing I'd learned something, anything at all about him."

I sighed.

Ben listened. He was oddly quiet.

I rolled over on my back and looked up at the sky. I closed my eyes for a minute. In a bit, I continued, "Papa told me he thought the gypsy's portrait was a perfect likeness of his Bertie."

I looked over at Ben. He'd rolled over. I thought he was asleep. He may have been crying. I knew not to ask. I let him rest for a while.

Maybe the man wasn't a real gypsy after all. Maybe he was a world famous painter who only disguised himself as a gypsy and traveled the world over creating his remarkable artwork. I recalled the painting of the beautiful brown-haired lady on the side of his wagon. Was it she who broke my gypsy's heart?

Aunt Mamie was right when she said I could come up with a story about most anything.

"Sleepy boy, come on! Are you going to waste the whole day?"

Ben stretched out his long and growing body. His arms went back over his head and his knees popped and cracked as he yawned. I giggled when I thought how Fred described Ben as a scarecrow. That afternoon my brother was a scarecrow, one who had blown over in the wind.

We rode up just as Papa was walking home from Fitch's. He had such a mournful look on his face, I feared something terrible had happened. My first thought was of Fred and Rebecca. I jumped from Maud's back and raced to meet him.

"Papa! What's wrong? I can see it on your face. Has something happened to Fred?"

"Oh no, darlin' girl." Papa put his arm around me. "But, come inside, there is something I must tell you."

My feet felt like railroad ties as I walked up the steps.

Papa motioned Ben into the back. "Put up the horse, son. I need a moment with your sister."

18

"What is it, Papa?"

He told me to sit down next to him on the settee. I was shaking all over. We never sat there and I knew it was serious. Papa took a letter from his pocket. I immediately recognized my aunt's handwriting. I choked up. Every face I knew in Asheville came into view the way pictures appear when someone flips fast through the pages of an album.

"Papa?"

"Ociee, I know how tender you are. It distresses me something awful to have to tell you this news. I am so sorry, so very sorry; but Mr. Lynch's Old Horse had to be put down."

"Put down!" I shouted. I was a farm girl. I knew at once my dear Old Horse was dead. I also knew he had been destroyed. Making my hands into fists, I pounded Papa's chest. Sitting in silence, he endured my attack.

"No, Papa! It's not true! Take it back!" I screamed until my throat throbbed.

Putting his arms around me, Papa pulled me in close to himself. He rocked me back and forth as if I were a tiny baby. I was totally unaware of how long we stayed that way.

I wasn't able to talk for gasping. Finally, I mouthed, "What happened?"

Papa spoke slowly, "Mamie wrote that they believe his tired old heart simply gave out. The poor animal stumbled and fell late in the afternoon. He couldn't get his legs back enough to stand up."

Papa looked down at the letter. He then took my hand. "Mr. Lynch confided to Mamie that the horse had grown weary as of late. He blames himself, says he should have realized it was time to put the Old Horse out to pasture. He just couldn't bring himself to do it."

"Old Horse won't ever have be put to pasture now," I sobbed. I asked to see the letter. Tears flooded into my mouth as I read Aunt Mamie's words.

At the end, she wrote,

And so, my dear brother, I am pained to ask you to break this tragic news to Ociee. However, I truly believe it is best for her to hear this from you. I would not want her to discover it upon her return next week. I send my love to you, to my darling Ociee, to Ben and Fred, and now also to Rebecca.

I am your devoted sister,
Mamie

Looking at the date on the letter, a shudder ran straight through me. Old Horse had died the Friday afternoon before Fred's wedding. I'd been so excited that day; my only concern was that I wouldn't fall on my face as I walked down the church aisle the next morning.

"Poor, poor Mr. Lynch!" I moaned. "Oh, Papa, can you imagine how sorrowful he was when they shot Old Horse? My heart aches to think about it."

"I know, dear, I know."

Once again, I reread the letter. I kept hoping to read it and find out it was all a big mistake, that Old Horse was going to be all right after all. But he wasn't. Old Horse was dead.

Midway though her letter, my aunt referred back to the trouble she'd had making up her mind about going with me to Mississippi.

As disappointed as I was about missing Fred's wedding, I am glad I was here to comfort George. He is doing better, a strong man is our dear George.

I sniffed. "Aunt Mamie says Mr. Lynch is going to be all right. Papa, the only thing I can think about is seeing that horse lying there in the street." My voice trailed off, and I started to cry again.

Ben burst in and announced, "Maud's fed and put up. What are we having for supper tonight?"

"You hush up, Ben Nash!" I yelled.

"What'd I do?"

Papa told Ben about Old Horse. He looked at me real sweet like. I could see Papa's own caring expression on my brother's face. "I'm so sorry about that horse, Ociee," he said softly.

I didn't feel a bit like supper that night. Papa said I didn't have to eat much, just a bite or two. I picked up a raw carrot, put a shawl around my shoulders, and walked out onto the kitchen stoop. The carrot wasn't cooked or cut up. I wanted to eat it just as it had come out of the earth. I pretended I was Old Horse, and I fed the whole thing to myself.

"I will miss you so much, my fine buggy horse. I know you well, and I know you wouldn't have liked being put out to pasture. And that's the truth of it." I looked up into the evening sky. "Are you up there pulling one of the Lord's buggies? Will you take Mama for a ride through the stars this night?"

I thought about our parade on January 1. And I remembered that silly hat. I was sorry I made Old Horse wear it. The memory did make me laugh for a second. Then I realized I'd never see him wear that hat again. I was about out of tears for one day. I wandered out into the yard.

Ben's cat walked out of the bushes and rubbed up against my leg. "You know, don't you, Tiger?" He followed me on out to the stable to see Maud. She was a plow horse, and looked nothing like Old Horse; but even so, the sight of her tugged at my heart. Tiger circled me once again and left me alone.

"Hello, Maud. I guess you're the only horse I really have left to love in this world." She reared her head and snorted into the cool air. I hurried back in the house and poured some sugar into the palm of my hand. Ben was getting his lessons for school. Papa was at his desk working. I didn't make a sound, because I didn't want them to bother me.

"Maud, I've not thought to give you this treat the whole time I've been home. I'm sorry for that. You've carried me all over this county for nearly a month, so it's time I thanked you." I held out my hand with the sugar. Her big pink tongue lapped it up. It tickled my hand and made me think of Old Horse. I could almost feel him. Did Maud sense my sorrow? Maybe she was just showing her pleasure for the sugar.

Her tongue tasted the last morsels that had melted between my fingers. The last time I'd treated Old Horse to sugar was just before Mr. Lynch and Aunt Mamie took me to the station. "I'll be back soon with your sugar and some carrots, too," I had promised him. I recalled patting his nose and looking into his soft black eyes.

Again, I looked into the sky. Where else would I look for him? I surely didn't think of him buried in the earth, and I couldn't think of what else would have become of his body. Maud finished her sugar, and I said goodnight to her. I turned around for one last look. I was beginning to realize that those I loved, even horses, seemed to go away when I wasn't looking.

Friday morning, Ben was at school and Papa was at Fitch's. I'd recorded Old Horse's death in my journal. The lines directly above those words had so happily described the wedding. Now these: *Ben and I came home from playing at the farm. Papa told me Old Horse died.*

I couldn't bear to put the date. I didn't want to remember. Why was it that bad things had a way of rubbing away my joy?

I decided to go by and call on Mrs. Hutchinson. I knew she was lonely what with Rebecca gone and the wedding festivities over with. Selfishly, I figured cheering her up might lift my own sorrow. Afterwards, I

planned to make myself write Aunt Mamie and Mr. Lynch. That was
going to be hard for me.

Mrs. Hutchinson greeted me at the front door. "Welcome, Ociee,
welcome to our home! Do come in," she chattered.

I followed her inside.

"I've been so busy this morning putting away the gifts." She
suggested that I sit down and watch. I offered to help, but she declined,
explaining that she had her own special way of doing things. As I
watched, Mrs. Hutchinson would continue to place something in a box,
only to take it out, then put it somewhere in the room, and finally put it
back in yet another box. "I declare, I am as busy as a bumblebee!"

Again I offered my help. Just watching her like that was making me
jumpy. Rebecca's mother simply ignored my offer.

"I am certain the young Nashes will soon travel to Abbeville to
gather these lovely presents for their charming home in Memphis." She
fumbled with some wrapping paper.

I couldn't answer quick enough before she added, "My dear, you
did look absolutely darling at the wedding. I know your father was ever
so proud of you and of your brothers, naturally!"

I did squeeze in a "thank you, ma'am" before she started to relive
the wedding, I guessed, probably for the one-hundredth time. My whole
visit went just like that, with her buzzing around the room and me sitting
and fidgeting. I hadn't said three entire sentences when I told her that I
really must be on my way.

Mrs. Hutchinson exclaimed, "My dear girl, I cannot begin to thank
you for your charming visit. You simply must come again! You are such
a delight. Do come back often. Oh dear, but you are leaving, too. Well
then, do return to us very soon. Yes, please do!"

I could breathe once I got a few houses away.

I stopped by Fitch's Mercantile. Papa greeted me warmly. Mrs. Fitch
came out from behind the counter and said how sorry she was to hear
about the loss of my friend's horse.

"Thank you, Mrs. Fitch."

I pulled on Papa's shirtsleeve. "I have an idea, Papa. Do you think I should give some silver coins to Mr. Lynch to help him buy a new horse?"

Mrs. Fitch heard me. "That is such a generous idea, Ociee! Bless your sweet soul."

"Our Ociee is a very kind young lady, indeed," beamed Papa. "Of course, dear, as I mentioned before, you should do with that money whatever you choose. I think it is a grand idea to help the fellow."

"Good!" I turned and ran out from the store. I hurried home to write the letter. It took me most of the afternoon, because the words had to be right. I'd write, tear up the paper, and start over again. Finally, I had what I wanted it to say.

Dear Mr. Lynch, also my dear Aunt Mamie,

You must be so sad. I understand, because I love Old Horse as much as I love any person, well almost. Mr. Lynch, I know Old Horse is in Heaven. You will see him again when you go there. Please do not go soon. I cannot bear to lose another person.

You know that two weeks ago, I found some silver that was buried during the War. I had planned to surprise Aunt Mamie and give her one fifth of it. However, I so much want you to feel better, and I know she would not mind what I am going to do. You see, there is plenty enough money, so that I now plan to give some to her, and also some to you to buy yourself a new Old Horse.

Love, Ociee

I got to the Post Office in time to get my letter posted. Mr. Sam called to me, "Aren't you George's daughter Ociee?"

"Yes, sir."

"Got some mail here for you folks. I was just getting ready to put it in your box, but if you can wait a minute, I'll give it to you now."

I was glad I was there. For along with some mail for Papa came a letter for me. I recognized Elizabeth's writing on the envelope. I tore it open and sat on the Post Office steps to read it.

Dear Ociee,

By now you know about our dear Old Horse. My heart is smashed to pieces. I am so sad about this. When I thought about how much you love that horse, my heart broke even more. I do not know what to say to cheer us up.

I will try. My father bought one of those motorcars. So far, Mother will not let me near it. Too dangerous! Father is thinking about letting Mr. Lynch try to drive it.

Also you do not have to buy me a present. I only want my friend to be back home. By the way, I told everyone at school about your treasure. You are famous.

Love, Elizabeth

A few days later, I was beginning to get my clothes organized for the trip home. I'd washed out some things and hung them on the line to dry. As I pinned then onto the clothes wire, I began to dread the long train ride back to Asheville.

As it was anytime I was getting ready to be some other place, I felt befuddled. I didn't want to leave, yet I wanted to get there fast as I could. This time was worse, because my Old Horse wouldn't be coming to get me. Even so, the crazy Ociee in me wouldn't allow myself to believe that horse wasn't going to be there. I had to see with my very own eyes before I'd know he was truly gone.

I went back in the house and opened my traveling bag.

It would be good to see everyone, especially Elizabeth and Aunt Mamie. I thought about the Murphys' motorcar. Mrs. Murphy was acting like a silly scaredy-cat. I surely hoped my aunt would permit me to go for a ride. Even more, I'd like to see the day Mr. Lynch was driving one, too. I could almost see myself sitting right there next to him.

There were a few things I could go on and pack. I gathered my wedding clothes. There'd be no need for them anytime soon.

The month with Papa and my brothers had gone by way too fast. I suppose that was because of the excitement of coming home, all the fun we had, and the wedding, of course. I wandered around in the house, waiting for Ben and Papa to get home. Fact was there was one more thing that needed my doing. I penned a quick note to Papa and Ben.

"Come on, Maud, you and I have one last trip to make. Saddle or not?"

The horse didn't seem to care, so I saddled her because it made for an easier ride. I had a couple of things to ponder without worrying about hanging on tight. We trotted out from town. The homes and businesses grew fewer and farther in between, and I began to enjoy more of the green of the land. Trees hung over the dirt road. I noticed that their leaves were starting to peek out from their winter cocoons.

Maud's feet clip-clopped along, and I sat back in her saddle.

19

In not too long a time, fifteen or twenty minutes or so, I turned Maud's reins toward the cemetery. I wanted to visit Mama's grave. I could remember the two pine trees and a large sweet gum near the spot, but I knew it might take me a while to find it on my own. I'd only come with Papa and hadn't paid attention.

I tied Maud in the shade at the base of a rise.

"You rest, girl. We can't be having anymore horses wearing out on us."

I climbed up the hill and began to wander through the graves. So many of the names I read on the headstones sounded familiar to me. It was as if I were walking up and down the streets in Abbeville or out amongst the farms where we used to live, and I was looking at all their names on fence posts.

Most of the names belonged to folks I knew, last names especially. Sometimes the first names were different, sometimes the same. I all but fell over in shock when I noticed the name "Ruby Hall" carved on one stone. Mrs. Hall had come into Papa's store just last week. I'd seen her at the wedding, too. Goodness, she had even talked to me! She was the wife of the Mr. Hall at the Abbeville train station, the kind man who was always so nice to us. On close inspection the dates read 1811–1854. I breathed a sigh of relief that my Mrs. Hall was alive.

I hoped mighty hard that I wouldn't be seeing "Ociee Nash" carved into one of those markers.

I thought I recognized the setting once and ran over to it. The same kinds of trees were there all right, but a different family was buried beneath them. "Brown" was written on their markers. I wondered if those folks were part of Ben's teacher's family. After all, I understood that most folks, even teachers, belong to other people. The sad thing is that death will always take people away from their families.

Aunt Mamie so often said, "Every person loses people they love. The true sorrow would be in never loving those people in the first place."

I wandered around among the other headstones and came upon a "Hutchinson," Edith E. Hutchinson, 1831–1899. She was Rebecca's grandmother. How tragic, I thought, she died before the wedding of her only grandchild.

A few plots over from the Browns, I saw "Fitch" on several markers. I had just begun to read the names when I spotted the daffodils Papa saved from Fred's wedding. Papa had arranged them in Mama's blue glass vase and brought them to her.

Susan Alberta M. "Bertie" Nash, 1853–1897
Beloved wife of George W. Nash

I touched the petals and noticed they had already turned brown. I became all the sadder. Mama would not have cared that the flowers were wilted. She'd say, "Why Ociee, those flowers are perfect!" Mama had a different way of thinking about things. Once she told me what she thought about a bouquet on our kitchen table.

"These posies are so much prettier than most, Ociee, because they came from Mrs. Fitch's garden." Her hand tenderly framing a single Black-eyed Susan, Mama added, "Her garden is such a bright and cheerful place; every flower from that spot carries along more joy than others might."

Mama enjoyed flowers in proportion to her closeness to the person who gave them to her. How she must have loved the flowers from Fred's wedding!

Susan Alberta M. "Bertie" Nash, 1853-1897
Beloved wife of George W. Nash

"I'm here, Mama, it's your Ociee. I've come with just me this time." I placed my finger on her stone and traced the letters of her name. B-E-R-T-I-E. I wished it had said "Mama" instead. My finger stayed for a time in the "1897."

Mama had been by herself in that cold place in the ground for more than three years. In my stomach, I could feel the horrid emptiness of that day.

I sat at her feet. "I still miss you, Mama. Tell me, will this hurting ever go away?"

I touched my locket, her locket. "Will it, Mama?"

I felt the burning of my tears as the long-trapped sadness welled up and demanded to be set free. "Will it ever stop? Can you hear me, Mama? Will it?"

Tears flooded my face.

Looking through my eyes was like watching out the kitchen window in the middle of an afternoon thunderstorm. This day, there was no storm. Not a single cloud scarred the sun-drenched crystal sky. Yet, I could barely see; and all I could feel was the pounding coming from deep inside my chest. There would be no crashing thunder to drown out the sound of my sobs.

I yearned to be with my mother, to touch her, to feel her arms around me, to be held by her.

No! That wasn't what I was feeling. I wanted to holler at Mama. Truth was, I was mad as I could be at her. I needed to scream at her for what she had done to me, for what she had done to our family. My whole body cried out for release.

But that would be a terrible thing to do, wouldn't it? I looked around the graveyard. No one was anywhere in sight, no one but me. Only the good Lord above would hear me. That wouldn't be right either; would it?

Yell at the Lord!

But why not?

After all, it was the Lord's fault that Mama was gone. Maybe He needed to get a piece of my mind.

I hadn't exactly decided about the Lord and me, when my whole insides exploded. "*Mama!* Why did you go away? *How dare you!*"

Birds soared from their branches; squirrels scampered high to the tiptops of the trees around her grave.

Susan Alberta M. "Bertie" Nash, 1853-1897
Beloved wife of George W. Nash

My throat closed tight as if to shut my mouth. Then slowly it opened and throbbed to the same beating as of my heart. I dropped to my knees at Mama's feet and wept.

Minutes must have passed. I didn't know for certain. I raised my eyes and blinked. Wet hair stuck to my forehead and cheeks. As I sat up, I licked my lips and tasted salt.

Then there was quiet.

"Ociee, girl, what are you doing?"

Ben. He was walking up the hill toward me.

Wiping my eyes on my sleeve, I jumped to my feet and hurried down the hill to meet him.

"Where did you come from, Ben? You about scared me to death."

To death…

"Saw your note," he said. "Hitched a ride on the back of a farmer's wagon."

I listened.

"Ociee, you been crying?"

"Some."

"I've never been back to this place before now," Ben admitted. "I didn't know exactly where to come, but I saw you from the road."

"Took me a bit of looking to find her spot."

"I just hated that day Mama was…," his voice trailed off.

Silently, I took my brother by the hand and led him back up toward Mama's grave. He held tight but kept coming with me. My hands were cold. His were sweating like he was working in the cotton field.

"I suppose it might sound dumb to you, but I came to tell Mama good-bye since I'm leaving. I've never been here all alone. Reckon today is something new for me, too."

Ben began, "Papa comes all the time. He used to ask me to join him. 'Spect I was pretty stubborn about that. Fred comes, too, when he visits from Memphis." My brother kicked a dirt clod.

"Ben, I was, well, I didn't act just right."

My brother looked at me but said nothing.

"I'm mad at Mama!" My words came out like spit. "Why'd she go and die like that, Ben?"

"Don't know, Ociee, but it makes me mad as h-e-l-l."

"Ben Nash, you better not spell that word, or one of these days, you'll find yourself going there."

Ben didn't pay one bit of attention to my warning. He hollered loud as he could, "Mama! I hate you for leaving us. You ruined our whole family. Look, you've made Ociee cry!"

Ben's face, red as cherries, washed itself in tears.

"Ben?"

"Get away from me, Ociee. I ain't crying!"

Ben reached down, picked up a rock and hurled it at the stone. "Dern measles! I hate you, measles, for attacking our Mama. Measles, you go to h-e-l-l."

I grabbed hold of a rock and threw it hard. The rock hit dead center the Nash name. "Those measles went after Bertie Nash, our Mama, and killed us all, killed our family, they did! To hell with the measles!" I didn't bother to spell it out.

Ben and I both flew into frenzy. We were throwing dirt and rocks and yelling to the top of our lungs. But when I went after someone else's bouquet, I thought about Mrs. Fitch's flowers. The bouquet could have been another person's joyfulness. I stopped.

Ben stopped, too.

"The truth is, all the being mad in the whole world doesn't give us back our Mama," I said. I dropped down on the ground.

Worn plum out, I 'spose we both were, my brother and I just sat there.

I watched as the spring winds stirred all that was green around us. I heard Maud snort down at the bottom of the hill. The sunshine warmed our faces, and I could feel the peace of the moment.

Then, as if I were talking to Mama on our side porch, I began, "I'm getting ready to go back to North Carolina in a couple of days. I don't want to leave here, but I also want to be there."

Ben stared ahead.

"I came here to visit and to tell you about your Ociee. Reckon I loss track of that for a few minutes, Mama. Guess I should say I'm sorry."

I told Mama about Elizabeth, about Aunt Mamie and her shop, and how I'd learned so much. I hoped she was proud of the way her Ociee was growing up. I didn't ask; I knew she was.

I wanted to believe Mama walked with me some of the time.

"Mama, I've fixed up the new house for Papa and the boys using your curtains and quilts. I've placed around your pretty things, too. You didn't want your treasures stored away in trunks, did you? Remember your cut glass vase? I keep flowers in it all the time. You always took pride in showing me what was beautiful, and you told me I would learn to appreciate such things. You probably didn't think I was paying much attention to what you were saying. I was, Mama."

When I told her about Aunt Mamie's pretty home, hoping she'd remember it from her days visiting there, I mentioned about how my aunt and I often talked about "Bertie and George" and their courting days.

"Mama, how will I ever have a first kiss without being able to tell you all about it?"

"Kiss!" Ben came to with that. "What are you talking about that mushy stuff for? Mama doesn't want to hear about that!" With that my brother made a wrinkled up face, poked his thumbs in his ears, and stuck out his tongue as far as it could go.

"Mama, as you can tell, your Ben is still the same silly Ben that he's always been. Can you see this face he's making? Mama, remember that you always laughed at us children?"

Ben hopped onto his knees and said, "Tell her, Ociee. Tell Mama about Fred's wedding!"

"Oh, Mama, Rebecca was so beautiful, and Fred was so handsome, just like Papa! I looked real pretty. I wore a pink dress that Aunt Mamie made 'specially for me."

"I looked nice, too, Mama!" said Ben, getting to his feet and talking louder than me. "I didn't complain, not once, about dressing up. Well, not much anyhow."

I rolled my eyes at Ben. "You know that's not true, Mama. Oh, Mama, when Fred made his promises to Rebecca, his knees were just shaking so much! Everyone in the pews could see his pants just flapping like our rooster's wings when he chased the chickens! Later, Papa told Ben and me that his own pants legs shook like Fred's during your wedding. Is that true, Mama? How I wish I could hear your answer."

Again came the quiet.

Susan Alberta M. "Bertie" Nash, 1853-1897
Beloved wife of George W. Nash

When I got sad sometimes, I started talking about anything that popped into my head. "Mama, did you know that Mr. Lynch, George

Lynch, is Aunt Mamie's beau? I 'spect Papa told you about him. Papa came all the way to Asheville to see what he thought about his sister's fellow. I like to say our family has two Georges these days."

I thought about Old Horse.

"Mama, if you should see a fine buggy horse trotting around in Heaven, will you please see that he gets a fat, delicious carrot? He belongs to Mamie's Mr. Lynch. His name is Old Horse. He'll know who you are, because I've told him all about my Mama."

Ben looked at me. "Ociee, let's go home."

I nodded.

"It's starting to get late, Mama. You know how Papa worries about us. Now, don't *you* be worrying about us children, or about Papa either. We are doing better every day."

Ben put his hand on the wedding flowers. "Bye, Mama. I'll come back again one day soon."

"Good-bye, Mama," I said. "I'm not mad anymore."

"Me, neither."

As we walked down toward Maud, I turned back. "Don't forget about the carrot for Old Horse."

Ben rubbed his eyes on the sleeve of his plaid flannel shirt, one Mama had made for Fred.

"Are you all right?"

"Yep."

"Think we can both ride home on Maud? She is saddled."

"Come on, Ociee," said my brother. "We Nashes can accomplish anything we set our minds to do."

Ben climbed on first and stretched out his arm to me. I gripped his hand, and he pulled me up onto Maud's back. As I turned around to take one last look, I thought I spotted a rider on a fine black horse atop the faraway hill. My gypsy? Just as quickly, he was gone.

A little wren flew up into the sweet gum tree.